Dating Blanche

by

Robin Jansen

Denton series

Cover Art by *Lea Schizas*

The Wild Rose Press, Inc.
PO Box 708
Adams Basin, NY 14410-0708
Visit us at www.thewildrosepress.com

Publishing History
First Edition, 2025
Trade Paperback ISBN 978-1-5092-6058-4
Digital ISBN 978-1-5092-6059-1

Denton series
Published in the United States of America

Dedication

Dedicated to Steven, my "eye-candy" who chauffeurs me to thrift shops and Saturday estate sales. Thank you for always carrying my load, both figuratively and literally

Special thank you to Lea Schizas, my wonderful editor, for her long hours and dedication to this book. You are the best.

Chapter 1

Simon Davenport
New Orleans

Simon Davenport found the place seductive despite the humidity that hung in the air like a wet towel. He meandered through the graveyards of New Orleans, photographing mausoleums, headstones, and statues, admiring the skill and artistry. Despite obvious beauty, it was already immortalized countless times making it overexposed and unoriginal—not what he needed.

A podcaster and blogger, Simon cultivated a dedicated audience of several hundred thousand followers over the years. Not enough to satisfy his ambition. Times sure had changed since he first got into the field. Right now, it felt like drowning in a sea of younger, fresher voices. What he needed was an award-winning book contracted with a renowned New York publishing house. The proposal was submitted to a top tier publisher months ago. That was his secret—at least for now. Between then and now, was a plethora of time for overthinking and playing guessing games which kept him on edge. Yes, or no: acceptance or rejection would calm his nerves.

The morning waned. Time to find a ripe story to feed his followers. 'A Man on the Street' type questions were in order hopefully opening new ideas to flood his creativity. With permission, he snapped photos of diverse people eager to share their thoughts.

Define love. What touches your soul? Is it possible to be in love with two people at once? If you never find love, what then? Is there something you have never told anyone? What are you are obsessed with? What's your favorite way to waste time? What is something popular now which annoys you? Tell me about your oldest friend and how you met? You get to relive one day of your life. Leave it be—or change it—how? Which day?

Strolling through a park, he spotted a dark-skinned girl—about kindergarten age—wearing a pink summer dress playing with her doll, while a woman sat close by. Her mother? Simon supposed.

"Hey, may I?" Simon asked, before seating himself at the far end of the bench.

"And you are?" She glanced quickly at her daughter.

"Simon Davenport." He handed the woman his card. "As you see, I have a blog and podcast. I am a safe person."

She read his card carefully then chuckled. "So this proves I should trust you. A bit of a braggart you are, Mister Davenport. Nice to meet you, just the same. I'm Mrs. Thornton. I'm sorry but I don't read blogs unless they are about recipes."

"No recipes." He shook his head and smiled.

"Well, then, what do you need from me?"

"I am a storyteller of sorts."

"Your genre?"

"I study love and how online dating affects us in today's modern world. I look for deep, dark, untold secrets."

"A love doctor with secrets. Now you have my interest. I might just take a listen sometime to your blog."

Simon felt his face flush. "Ah, a blog is read. I think you would enjoy listening to my podcast, Dating Blanche."

"I look forward to it."

"In your opinion, what form of love is the truest?" He pulled out his cell, and held it up. "May I record our conversation?"

With a nod and a laugh, her painted red, full lips parted, revealing perfect white teeth. "Well, Mister Davenport, you do ask the hard questions."

"You don't have to answer." He stood.

"You sit right back down. Give me a moment to think, will you?" She gazed into the distance and back at her daughter. "Agape. It's the truest."

"Explain?" Humidity formed beads of sweat drip down his back making his shirt stick to his skin. It was uncomfortable.

"Agape love is not dependent on the other person to do or to be anything. They don't need to love back. Love that just is freely given. No requirements."

"Like the love for a child?" Simon watched the little girl drop her doll, then pick it up to brush it off.

"Like the love of a child. Or the love of a cruel mother who rejects her children." She sighed. "They do nothing to earn your love. You just love."

"Sounds like you've known rejection."

"Now that's too personal. But it happens. Or when you fall in love, and they don't feel the same. You can get mad and yell. Cry. Or you can just love anyway but move on. Acceptance." She shrugged her shoulders.

"Agape is the truest form. No requirements. No conditions. But if you need more than they can give, leave."

"I've never heard anyone speak of love in that way. Thank you. May I?" He held up his camera.

"Yes. But let me pose us." She pulled her daughter toward her, then turned their backs to the camera with only the doll facing forward. It was an interesting shot; one Simon wouldn't have thought to take.

Finished, he showed the mother the shot.

"This is great. Thank you." She smiled.

"I am glad you approve." Simon reached for his wallet.

Mrs. Thornton refused payment.

Despite the heat, Simon decided to walk a path past an old cemetery where two elegantly dressed elderly women with silver hair, strolled arm in arm. Only one held a parasol due to the sun's rays. Simon was certain they'd have many interesting stories to tell, so he jerked on the heavy, decomposing gate to open, then followed them for several yards before speaking.

"You two look like quite the pair," he said, immediately feeling silly over his choice of words.

"We are quite 'the' pair," one of the women responded, pulling back a piece of errant hair. "What you see before you are identical twin sisters. She's Betty and I'm Maggie. And you are?"

"Simon."

"Welcome, Simon," Betty said with a deep Cajun drawl. "I can tell by your accent you are not from these parts."

"No, ma'am. Texas."

Maggie interjected, "Never mind. We will talk to

4

you anyway."

"Come, along. Walk with us. Today we are laying these lovely flowers on our parents' graves."

Simon hadn't noticed the bouquet of fragrant gardenias until mentioned.

"But most importantly of all, we are going to spit on the graves of our past lovers," Maggie snickered.

"What?"

"Oh, don't listen to my sister," Betty said with a lift of her shoulders. "We're not spitting on anything. But we may just dance on their graves." Her lips widened into a mischievous grin.

"That I'd love to see." Simon held up his camera.

"Come on then." They beckoned.

They placed the bouquets on their parents' graves followed by silent prayers. Crossing themselves, they turned in the opposite direction. Simon did his best to keep up with the elderly ladies while photographing their antics from behind. They giggled hurrying along, giving one another little shoves and recalling funny memories.

Ten graves in all, they danced, then curtseyed as though it had been a special performance then onto the next crossed-over lover. Simon rapidly took dozens more pictures of the uninhibited, expressive sisters, capturing their fun.

At lunch, Simon listened to antidotes about dating.

"We were known as 'the package deal'." They looked one another in the eyes as they cracked up like co-conspirators.

"We only dated men who were also good friends with one another," Betty explained. "That way we double-dated and had so much more fun together while we didn't have to pay for a thing. But if one of us gals lost interest, we'd break off with both."

Maggie continued. "One evening I was seated in the front next to my beau who was driving. Betty was in the backseat with her beau."

"I was wearing a black cocktail dress."

"You looked smashing."

"Thank you. And I often think about the gaberdine jacket you wore."

"And he asked her to marry him."

"The ring was beautiful," Betty admitted with a smile.

"But Betty told him 'no' because…" Maggie looked at her sister with a smile.

"Because Maggie was about to break it off with her beau."

"We always had so much more fun with each other's company that we never married."

"I know, it sounds heartless but most of the men we found boring or mean. So, we dance in remembrance of our time together."

The stories were usable.

Simon paid for lunch. Afterwards they exchanged goodbye hugs while quarreling about which one should date Simon.

"You are way too old for him," Betty protested to her sister.

"What do you mean by that? I am the youngest of the two," Maggie said.

Simon laughed. "You both are too much for me. I don't want you dancing on my grave."

To escape the heat of the day, Simon cruised along in his car, AC blasting, searching for—something more.

That special moment that captured emotion, propelling people to post their thoughts online and discuss his blog during their office break. He'd already been here for a month, and had enough stories, but not the one that would take him up a notch. Get him noticed. Who was he kidding? He wrote fluff. Maybe it was time to hit the interstate back to Texas.

Simon silently said goodbye to the delicious eateries, the unique jazz players, the delightful tourists, and the colorful natives along the narrow streets. This was the last hurrah; if nothing turned up today, he'd be in his own bed by midnight.

The traffic was terrible. Simon dodged the onslaught of cars and turned into a narrow side street with tight twists and turns. Around another corner, the street opened just a bit, where his eye caught sight of an amazing historic building. The tires crunched on the gravel as he turned into the parking lot, riddled with gouges and cracks. Curious, he pulled the camera strap over his shoulder and got out of his mustang. As Simon walked toward the old church, he admired the patched brick walls—gabled windows—climbing ivy. Tall Hollyhocks remained in stately rows beneath the sills behind a fleur-de-lis iron fence.

Camera ready, he carefully navigated through the underbrush, making sure not to trip. The church, bramble hedge, and red stone looked like it would taste of cinnamon if you licked it. The closer he got, the more interesting the old decorative trims appeared. Voices came from the direction of the steps. Inside, an organ played religious music. It'd be cool to take a picture or two of a southern funeral.

Not wanting to be seen, he glanced about to find an

obscure place to lurk. Feeling like an interloper, Simon knew he should leave, but his curiosity was too great. He stood where the brush hadn't been cleared for perhaps years. It was then he saw her for the first time.

Ginger-haired Rapunzel leaned there, against the stone, as though she had just escaped the tower to meet her prince. She gazed at the treetops. What was she searching for? Some divine answer? He never believed in fairy tales until now.

At that moment, she jerked with surprise seeing him stare at her. Ready for flight, he had to stop her. "Excuse me, but may I photograph you, right there? Just as you are. Please."

She took a small step forward.

"No, don't do that. Don't move." He lifted the camera.

She looked down at her clothes, a cotton dress, an old sweater, bare legs, and sandals. A painful confused expression crossed her face, but obediently she settled against the church again. As if on cue, tears rushed into her eyes. His lens caught all this bundled emotion and hoped this moment would translate. He'd title this offering, Magic of the Moment.

Simon took a series of shots. Tendrils of her hair floated in the breeze. The ruffle of her dress covered her ample hips and large bust. A spray of freckles crossed her nose and then disappeared into a powdered face. "Hello. I am Fiona." Her voice seemed a whispered promise.

"I'm Simon. You are beautiful. "It was then Simon felt sure he had a story and now had a reason to stay in NOLA longer.

His cell rang, interrupting this moment.
Alice.

Chapter 2

Alice 20 years old
Eau Claire, Wisconsin
38 years earlier…

On the first day of Advanced Art Form, the male model briskly crossed the room with long self-assured, barefooted strides. He slipped from his robe and hiked himself up on the tall stool. Parting his legs, a large male organ bushed forward.

"Oh gawd," someone whispered as other students softly giggled. A few more coughed.

Bravely, Alice raised her hand. "Um, isn't this Intro to Caricature Drawing? I thought I signed up for *that* class." Alice Rigby's voice trailed as she scanned the room, hoping for someone, anyone, to nod their head in agreement.

"This is advanced art for serious art majors," someone blurted.

Trying to cover her anxiety, she struck a thoughtful posture and focused on a ceiling tile as she gathered courage to draw. Once the awkward feeling of surprise passed, she slowly lifted her eyes to take a second look at his large jewels but started at the toes where the nails were nicely groomed. Next Alice's examination focused on his knees knowing she was only mere inches away from what she wanted most to see.

Traveling upward, her eyelids fluttered as she chickened out and her gaze landed on his face. Certainly the nude had a strong bone structure with a slight left lean in the center of his nose.

Alice knew his unexpected rude chuckle was meant for her so she slipped on an invisible mask of nonchalance to hide her nervousness and took a gulp of air. Rapidly she sketched, pretending this wasn't the first time seeing male genitals. Of course, there were pictures in books and statues in art museums she had seen. But it was so much different in the flesh.

Being good at cartoon figures, meant she was good at reinterpretation. She sharpened her attention on the unspeakable, but prolific, aspect of the nude's frame and neutralized it, by re-envisioning the mass of wiry curls as a ball of angora yarn that her steely-haired grandmother pulled from to knit herself a shawl. The genital was drawn as an old woman's hand. If the model returned tomorrow, she'd reimagine him as a bowl of fruit with an apple that Eve would eat.

When class ended, the model caught Alice by the arm, momentarily stopping her work. "Catch coffee with me?"

"Ahh-hhh—you want me to catch coughing, er—I mean, you said coffee—right? With you?" Alice stammered slightly confused. She supposed he had a nice face, but all she recalled were his baseball-sized, dangling genitals. "I can't."

"Okay." He strode off toward another female student. "Hey, babe, how about some coffee."

"Oh, is that what it's called these days," the girl swooned. "I'm game."

"Okay, Gamey."

Although she had another class, Alice lingered over her drawing. The art professor observed Alice's technique as she sketched. "Perhaps, you should switch to another form of art."

Alice immediately thought of another artist and his thoughtful paintings focusing on the simplicity of life. "Andrew Wyeth?"

"No, not him, unless you are speaking of hanging his picture, not creating one. I suggest you switch your concentration a different art form."

"Oh?" Alice asked.

"Either you are good at drawing, or you aren't. It's all in the technique. You like modern reinterpretation more than realism. Perhaps, outdated home décor or outrageous fashion design would make you more comfortable," he snipped.

Alice considered his suggestion. She did enjoy rearranging her apartment furniture. She loved spending afternoons gazing at paint chips at the major paint stores. By golly, her professor had to be right. And with that, her life tumbled in a new direction, creating room-by-room designs featuring repurposed furniture. It irrevocably changed her course, and again set sail, satisfied life had placed her on the right path. Interior design.

Chapter 3

Denton, Texas
38 years later...

Alice stood naked in front of the bathroom mirror; the steamy aftermath of her shower still floated in the air. Thick, gray curls cascaded around her shoulders. They were the best part of her looks. It was impossible not to notice the changes in her older body that had taken root. After all, she was more than halfway to the finish line, glad there wasn't a steady man to analyze each imperfection, let alone talk about it. To soothe the absence of a lover, she told herself this was not a good time in life to be naked in front of anyone.

Fifty-plus-eight was more than a number. It was fighting high cholesterol, turkey neck, arthritis, lunch lady arms, and facial lines. The macaroon she ate last week had found its way to her hips with all the other pastries she nibbled on from time to time. How she wanted sinewy, perfectly toned arms and a flat tummy along with another hot fudge Sunday. "Yeah, and just toss in a million dollars, please."

Alice wrestled into her jeans, buttoned her blouse, and added Navajo turquoise earrings. Unlike her former twenty-something self—this single Alice Rigby knew where she was going—and today that was to a Dallas estate sale to glean inventory for her shop, *Alice's*

Rabbit Hole of Design.

Excitement bubbled. Rocketing south on I-35, the speedometer bounced above 90. Up ahead a road crew worked. She tapped her brakes to avoid acquiring another ticket. Those things were getting expensive.

It was April. Thanks to the former First Lady, Ladybird Johnson's love for the state flower, billions of bluebonnets now carpeted Texas. It provided the perfect backdrop for couples, children, babies, and dogs to be photographed on fields of blue. *Just watch out for those rattlers hiding in the grass.*

Alice eyed them with slight envy. Family, that is not snakes, although family could also be snakes. Traffic picked up along with the freeway noise. Alice rolled up the window to listen to the radio.

The foray into the Highland Park area of Dallas was wildly fruitful—and today was better than she had hoped. Not only was she the first through the front door, but the high-end estate sale turned out to have low-end price tags of antique furniture. She scored and filled her white SUV with the most amazing treasures; a 19th Century Storr Sterling Tea Set, French Mop Opera glasses, boxes of Flow Blue dishes, a small cache of Native American jewelry and Kittinger arts, and a few pieces of crafts furniture. The worry of someone else getting there before her made last night's sleep impossible. Greed was what capitalism was all about, right? And so was the key to her dream of home ownership in a historic section of her town, Denton, Texas.

The familiar ping from a text drew her attention. Alice carefully swerved her car to an exit ramp and found a place to stop. It was a bit of a surprise to find she had missed so many including the latest from Simon Davenport, her dearest, longtime friend, Simon. Simon. She located his number in her favorites and pressed call.

"What's up?"

"Alice, we need to talk."

"And a hello to you, too. I tried calling you several times. You never answered. You must have lots of stories to tell with all the time you spent away." There was something off with him.

"Hi. Sorry. Yeah, I was busy."

"Did you get my latest dating disaster email for your column?" she asked, hoping to way-lay the terrible news she suspected. "I emailed it days ago. If you didn't, check your spam folder. I saved it, so I can always resend. By the way, you are going to love writing this next week's column for 'Dating Blanche'. This one sounds like a real charmer. He's from East Texas and raises snakes and milks their venom. Get it? Snakes. Charmer. Snake charmer?"

"Yeah, cute." He pressed on, "I have incredible news to share."

"What?"Alice held her breath.

"I'll tell you when I see you."

How she wished she could yank the 'incredible news' out of him but pulled herself together. "Great. When will that be?"

"I got in last night."

"Oh. You don't give me much warning, do you?" She laughed. "How about a hamburger for lunch?"

"I'll see you in forty minutes."

"Make that an hour."Alice removed her glasses and tucked them back into the pocket of her purse. Mixed emotions stirred. It was confusing. First, there was joy and anticipation over seeing Simon. She always looked forward to working together with him on the latest 'Dating Blanche'—she thought of it as her Hollywood name. Using a pseudonym provided anonymity.

A pang of nerves rumbled. What was Simon about to say? The thought of him with someone else constantly niggled in her mind and this trip he had been gone two months, longer than usual. Every time he took a work trip, she feared he'd return with a lover. Putting on a look of happiness would be difficult, but she was determined to do so if it came to that. Occasionally, she practiced her look of surprise and happiness for him in the mirror. Their friendship was good and steady. An attempt to blurt out her love for him would ruin it. In the meantime, she played sad songs of unrequited love over and over.

For now, she'd look on the bright side. Number one, Simon was finally back in town. Number two, daughter Zeba was engaged. Practice gratefulness was her new mantra.

Alice parked at the rear of her shop. Nick, the high school weekend help she hired along with Stella, her assistant, would see to emptying the SUV.

Nick was the kind of kid who said exactly whatever came into his head. Stella acted as though she had been in the middle of a midlife crisis that lasted for the last twenty years. Stella's eyes were set far apart, and her high forehead begged for bangs. The woman's dark hair framed her pretty face with lips that always looked pouty.

"What's up?" Alice asked.

"There's a rat caught in a trap outside on the

sidewalk."

"Tell Nick to handle it."

"I do believe you hit a goldmine this morning. You really should get a truck."Stella switched gears as she peeked into boxes.

"Hey, you look like you're in pain." Nick carried two captain chairs into the space, one in each hand. "It's probably sciatica. My grandpa has it."

"Your grandpa, huh? Thanks. Now, I'm feeling even older."

Nick turned red-faced. "Sorry, I didn't mean to make it sound like you were old. It's just that he complained about it the other night. I think he's way older than you. He just turned fifty."

"You better stop while you are ahead, Nick." Stella arched a brow.

"I'm meeting Simon for lunch. I'll be back afterward. Meanwhile, I'm taking this box of jewelry with me to mark."

"Wow, jewelry again. I hope turquoise. It does so well."

"It is. Native American."

"After you pick, I want a look," Stella called before bolting across the floor to help a customer open a sticking door.

Slowly, Alice climbed the narrow, steep steps. Above her shop, was a five hundred square foot loft that was home. The space only permitted a few pieces of utilitarian furniture like a pullout couch, a dresser, and a linoleum table with two mismatched chairs. An odd assortment for being a connoisseur of valuable antiques. But first came the house, then she'd fill it to the brim with everything she loved.

After a quick shower, she eased into a freshly laundered pair of loose-fitting cotton capri's and slid into a green top to bring out the green in her own eyes. Tugging the scrunchie from her ponytail, Alice ran a brush through her curls then reapplied powder to her face, adding a bright pink blush to her cheeks and a sweep of red lipstick. She kissed the air in front of the mirror. Thankfully, lipstick made a positive difference with her complexion. *Every woman needs to always carry of tube of red on her.* She dug through her estate sale jewelry and selected a large turquoise sterling Native American Manasa ring to slip onto her finger and the turquoise Nevada Royston cuff onto her wrist. Those she'd keep.

The restaurant was blocks away, yet she refused to give in to the pain and decided to walk. Lumbering along, her pants felt tighter—obviously skipping the gym three months didn't do her thickening waistline any favors along with the nightly candy she ate in bed.

Alice sat at the booth watching the clock. Waiting. Waiting. Simon was nearly twenty minutes late. Lateness. It was his thing. It was always "hurry, hurry, Alice" and then he turned up late with some lame excuse. The man never bothered with time, except when it came to his fanatical self-imposed deadlines. No matter, she'd wait and eat garlic bread sticks, while checking her account page on the dating site. Dating online was research for Simon's blog. Of course, he never used her real name. Together they came up with a pseudo name for her. Thus, Blanche was born. It was fun to overhear comments about Dating Blanche blog and Podcast. Dating over fifty was a popular thing. Even more fun that no one guessed what her side job was.

Ah. Her virtual dating mailbox was full. Which person should she focus on this week?

The waitress placed a pitcher of iced tea and a small bowl of pine nuts on the table.

"What can I get for you?"

"Nothing right now. Waiting for a friend." Alice nibbled at the nuts as the waitress left.

Feeling queasy again about Simon's news, Alice tapped her foot and peered out the window to check for a red sports car, his indulgence. Her thoughts fluttered back years.

Simon, the nude model who posed for the class with such flair. They laughed about it now. Later when they met again in journalism class, they did end up going for coffee.

Chapter 4

Eau Claire, Wisconsin
38 years earlier…

The spring semester started in the heavy snow of Wisconsin winter. Alice wore her signature outfit of jeans with a button-down blouse and a pullover red sweater, a black faux mink coat, and boots. She couldn't remember what he wore during that encounter, but his gaze was open and direct. By then Simon Davenport's way of making money for tuition was more conventional. He had gone from a popular nude to a popular bartender. He also became the president of the student body and ran the campus newspaper too. Right after graduation, he became a feature editor with a small New York magazine—moving from one employer to the next, always traveling up the journalistic ladder. He wrote human interest stories that drew attention and won independent awards. That's how 'Man on the Street' started. And usually wrote about love. Something Alice felt he was devoid of feeling.

While Simon crossed the country in search of fresh stories, Alice, who had yet to find herself, crossed the street to church to walk down the aisle to a man who had yet to find himself. Afterward, her area of concentration was housewifery to Thomas. Maybe she wasn't exactly that but when she had Zeba, she was a great stay-at-home mom. A few years later, both she and Thomas felt their marriage was a sham. By then Alice had enough of icy winters and frigid Thomas. She moved out of their three thousand square foot house, and they jointly filed for divorce. No fault.

Once the divorce was final, much to her parents' chagrin, Alice took Zeba and moved south to a sweet little town in Texas by the name of Denton where she finished her college degree in design. Eventually, Simon decided to make it his hometown, too since he now could work from anywhere as a podcaster and blogger.

Alice knew she wasn't any good with men—none of them stuck. Maybe it was because she always fell for the men who were remote; emotionally unavailable, like her dad. In fact, her healthiest male relationship turned out to be with Simon, whose biggest takeaway was he never seemed romantically interested in her again.

Chapter 5

Present Day

"Simon, where are you?" she whispered, looking around. Right on queue, he walked through the door. The word that came to her mind when she saw him was *home*.

Dressed in a pair of faded jeans and a pullover shirt, he stared at her. His eyebrows, dabbed with gray, formed a cloud-like appearance over the brow of his angular face. His shock of salt-and-pepper hair, swept back toward one side of his head, revealed the start of a receding hairline. Russet eyes, tinted with the history of all he had seen, peered through wire-rimmed glasses set on a narrow nose; his mouth turned upward in a generous grin. His manner exuded urgency. Simon was a tad over sixty and still immune to all Alice could offer—like loft living, morning green tea, and a hell of a good time.

"Sorry I'm late. Lost track of time." He kissed the top of her head.

"Welcome back." It felt good to be with Simon again. They had a closeness that grew with time.

His presence filled her with butterflies—or maybe it was the pine nuts she just ate giving her a bit of gas. Or could it be the garlic sticks?

Simon set his camera equipment carefully onto the

back of the table against the wall before sliding into the booth.

"Oh good, bread sticks." He grabbed one and took a bite.

Alice reflected that Simon wasn't so different from when she first met him. There was this windblown, half-rugged look about him, like he had just jumped a train bound for glory and was shocked to have made it aboard. His eyes captured the mischievous side of his personality. His full head of hair made him look younger than his years. His energy was compact. In a way, that man was the most amazing man she had ever known.

The waitress took their hamburger order with fries. Alice removed her reading glasses and turned them upside down on the table.

Except for the waistband on her jeans that pinched, and her throbbing toes that needed a massage, her attention turned to Simon. Earlier, he seemed anxious to talk, but now, an uncomfortable silence fell between them. She waited for him to finish the breadstick, only to reach for another. Why was he stalling?

Of course. Simon had to have met someone. The lunch invitation was about telling her. She hoped he didn't gush. That would be so unlike him. The new girl most likely was in her twenties and probably played some instrument like a trumpet while wearing a red bustier instead of a blouse. The very thought of losing Simon was like a stiletto through her heart.

All these years, never having been married, or even engaged, *why now Simon*? She imagined him standing at the altar, eyes lit with lust, as the flirty woman sashayed down the aisle blowing kisses at him.

It was impossible to hide her grief, so she tucked an errant strand of hair behind an ear and managed to brace herself for his response. "Okay, I'm listening." She took a breath and folded her hands on the table.

Simon looked her in the eyes. Finally, he spoke. "This is hard."

Tears welled. *Just say it. Get it over with.*

"Something happened while I was gone."

I knew it. Taking too deep of a breath, she swallowed air which sent her into a choking frenzy. Her eyes began to well with tears, spilling down her cheeks. There goes the column about Blanche, her life as it was with Simon—and their luncheons, such as they were—all done.

Simon pushed his glass of water toward her. "Are you okay?"

Alice nodded and patted her chest, doing her best to stop coughing. She took several sips of water from his glass. "Better. What were you saying?"

"While I was gone, right in the middle of writer's block, I was hit with this great idea."

"Let's hear it." Alice held her breath.

"It's about you."

"About me?" A bit startled, but in a good way, Alice didn't suppress her abrupt smile.

"Yes, I want to do a full story about you—actually more than a blog—more than a podcast."

"What more could there be?" She blinked with surprise as the bubble burst about the NOLA hussy. "You've already columned hundreds of stories about me, okay, dozens of stories about me."

"This is totally different."

"How so?"

"It's about you and your life. This town. Zeba. And finding love."

"Ah. Finding love. You're referring to my online dating?"

"Adventures. They've been on public display for a few years. The blog is popular because you are one interesting gal. Readers love you. Let's give them more of you."

"I think it all has more to do with how you write those stories. They always end with a laugh or a warm fussy." She handed back the compliment along with his glass of water.

"You know what my favorite one was?"

"Ray." She folded her hands together.

"Yes!"

"It seems to be everyone's favorite." Alice agreed. "He never gave a heads-up over being homeless."

"Who would suspect that would even happen?" Simon asked the rhetorical question.

"Not me."

"I remember you saying, at first glance, you wondered why his clothes were mismatched. Red scrub pants and a striped nylon top."

"It confused me because he said he was in real estate. It just didn't fit between what he said and what I saw."

"He worked late at night, right?"

"Yes. Turned out his job was cleaning a real-estate office at night and sleeping on a couch in an office. I bet he used an office computer to make contact." She drummed her fingers across her teeth in thought. "I never thought to ask at the time. Wish I had."

"When he offered you dinner from the dumpster,

instead of a restaurant, he seemed so vulnerable, so pathetic, and you won all the readers' hearts when you actually ate with him." Simon's voice filled with admiration.

"It was a dinner invitation."

"How could you do something like that? Eat food from a dumpster."

"I couldn't insult him by refusing, could I? Besides, the food was still in a takeout box, and looked clean. I examined it. My mother raised me right and taught me to be polite no matter the circumstances. However, I did offer to take him to dinner at a nice restaurant, but he preferred to arrange the plans for our date himself."

"You humanized him. You saw him. You made him feel important because of your kindness. A nurturer. That's what you are."

"Nice of you to say. Fast forward, he was able to secure housing and has a job."

"Eating out of a dumpster with a homeless man. Who could make this stuff up?"

"With me, there is no need for fabrication. I liked how you went on to write about the plight of the homeless to make the public more aware of the need for good housing. And…."

"What?"

"The thing is, Simon, all these guys I go out with have no idea it's going into a blog. Doesn't that make this faux dating?"

"Ha!" He laughed. "Faux dating. An interesting insight, but while on one of these 'faux dates', as you refer to them, you might find someone who interests you, someone you want to see more than once.

Someone who lights up your life. There is a goal in all of this. To find you a husband."

"I've already had that. There was one—I—did see—more than once." She looked at him from the top of her lids, feeling her cheeks heat with shame. She cupped her hands around her mouth to whisper, "Don't you remember?"

"Oh, that's right—Jack. You did like him. I am so sorry." Simon scooted forward in the booth to reach across the table and touch her face. "Wish I could wipe that humiliation away. It's okay."

"No, not okay. After two months of dating, how could I have guessed he'd get back with his ex the very next day?"

"The day after you two—consummated the relationship."

"Stop. I refuse to discuss it." She waved away the sexual recollection as she dabbed at her eyes with a small, square paper napkin.

"Seems a little suspicious to me that he'd dump you the day after—"

She shushed him as the waitress delivered their hamburgers along with a side of fries. Once she walked away, Simon said, "I'd love to tell that jerk just what I think of him."

"Maybe it wasn't his fault but mine. Perhaps I wasn't any good. Most likely I drove him away with my sexual ineptness back into the arms of the lady who hated sex. Her sex was better than mine, obviously. Thinking about it makes me feel bad about myself. I can't talk about it anymore." Alice shivered with a crushing sense of shame. But she was lonely, and she had liked this guy a lot—and it had been a while. So

27

long, she had forgotten what it was like to be someone. At that moment, she longed to remember how wonderful sex could be. But it didn't turn out wonderful. It turned out reprehensible.

"It's okay. I am sure you were just fine. And as for rushing things, we all lack judgment from time to time." Simon got up and slid in next to Alice. He wrapped his arms around her and held her tightly against him.

She felt safe; reassured that she wasn't a loose woman, after all. Simon smelled like a book dipped in cologne and garlic. She choked, "Never will I make that mistake again."

"No, you won't make that mistake again. But it's okay if you do." He held her tighter and kissed her forehead.

Someone poked her shoulder.

Chapter 6

"Mom, Simon. I didn't know you two would be here. Is everything okay? Mom, what's wrong?"

"Zeba!" Simon quickly released Alice and returned to his seat. "Sit next to your mom."

"We are both fine, honey. Just reminiscing." Alice quickly dried her tears and gave a perky smile as she patted the vacated space.

"I stopped to get my weekly Texas Pick 3 lotto tickets next door when I walked by the window and saw you." A young red-headed woman, with the angular elegance of a dancer, held the tickets between her freshly manicured fingers. Zeba lifted her narrow shoulders in her usual breezy manner. She kicked off her shoes and sat next to her mother. Zeba helped herself to the fries.

"I was just about to pitch a new idea to your mom."

"Great. I came just in time. Simon, you write the best love advice column I've ever read. And your podcasts about Mom's dates are hilarious. I just wish she'd be more careful. I worry she could end up getting really hurt by some psycho."

"I make sure that I am perfectly safe at all times."

"Oh yeah? What about the guy who took you to a steak house and groped you under the table?" Zeba asked.

"Well—that was the exception, but I got out of that

one just fine."

"By pretending you were about to vomit." Zeba rolled her eyes.

"I wasn't pretending."

"And you couldn't find the backdoor, so you ran into the restaurant's kitchen asking for the way out," Simon said, laughing.

"Oh, wasn't that the date when the cook helped you climb out the back window?" Zeba asked.

"But the best part was when she actually crawled under the bay of windows, so he wouldn't see her get back to her car." Simon laughed. "All while wearing a dress."

"I succeeded too," Alice said. "Although I did make a mess of my knees."

"I used that date to warn women what to do in order to be safe."

"I am helping women my age to know what they are facing out there. It ain't pretty but can be funny."

"Except for that scary one," Zeba said.

"A few scary dates."

"Her experiences. My words. Together—Alice and I make magic."

"We do. It's magic. Go ahead, Simon, tell us this new, wonderful idea of yours." It was all she needed to hear as she swirled the cubes around in her water glass. Confidence grew. Someday they would be together as a couple.

"It's more than a dating episode. I want to grow from that base. I'm talking about something more in-depth, more personal." Simon appeared serious.

"Ah, more personal. Nope." Alice backpedaled.

"I haven't even told you about it yet."

"Oh yes, you just stated it's 'more in-depth and more personal'."

"Alice, I didn't want to tell you this, but my career has taken some hits lately."

"You've won awards. You have hundreds of thousands of readers." Alice leaned toward him. "And your monthly podcast has hit an all-time high."

"Most have close to a million readers. I am small potatoes these days. Times have changed. What I have can evaporate just like that! I am an old, tired voice. It's time to up my game. My last two human interest stories weren't of interest to anyone. I ran a dozen ideas past my editor, and he only liked one." Simon raised his brows and sat back.

"Really? Tell me about the one." Alice leaned forward.

"You."

"You're kidding."

"I couldn't find a fresh story on my trip to New Orleans. Listen, I need your help."

"But you were gone for two months. What kept you?"

Surely, he'd pull out of this slump without her help. Yet, there was a huge part of her that wanted to help; she would always be there for Simon. Suddenly, a fire lit her from the inside out, flaming her face. *Damn menopause*. She finished the entire glass of water within seconds and then finished Simon's. Next, she fanned herself with a menu.

"Not to change the subject, Simon, but look what happened while you were gone!" Zeba flayed her fingers as she jiggled her hand at Simon.

"Wow! That's quite a sparkler." Simon whistled.

"Congratulations to you and Martin, the chef. When's the wedding?"

Zeba wiggled in her seat, beaming with excitement. "February of next year. We all need to go out together soon—how about Martin cooks for us at our place on his night off?"

"It's a date. But make it later in the summer. Your mother and I are about to take a trip together." He nudged Alice's foot with his under the table.

Alice jumped. "We're what?"

Simon took a huge bite of hamburger and then wiped a dollop of ketchup from his chin. He crumpled his napkin and playfully batted it across the table at Alice. "You need a vacation. I'm sure I owe you one, maybe two, by now."

"If you owe me a vacation or two, then I say, Venice and Rome!" Alice tossed the napkin back into his face.

"I was thinking closer to home."

"Will I even get out of Texas?" Alice didn't care where they went. She realized she would soon be alone with Simon on a trip.

"Simon, Mom might feel better about this proposition..."

"Proposal."

"Proposal, when she hears your pitch," Zeba prodded.

"Okay." Simon looked from Zeba to Alice. "People want to revisit their past to find out what might have been."

"Not me. The present keeps me plenty busy."

"Didn't you tell me, a while ago, that you are in touch with several of your past boyfriends?"

"From high school. A few from college." She winked at him.

"We've heard about your recent online dates, as amusing as they were. Only this is different. This is what class reunions are all about. Did the popular prom queen get fat? Is the captain of the football team bald? Has the class clown turned into a comedic genius? And is the class geek rich? And am I over that special guy who broke my heart? Did I make a mistake in not marrying him?"

Alice blurted, "Or did I make a mistake in marrying him? The answer is yes. Ops, sorry Zeba."

"No problem." She narrowed her eyes.

"And who said anything about a class reunion?"

"You belong to three sites. The first two sites are for dating over fifty, right? You meet strangers online who might turn out to be the love of your life."

"Hasn't happened," said Alice, biting into her burger angrily while wondering if he wanted to cut her loose.

"You sure are hungry," Simon observed.

"Or someone who turns out to be not who you think he is." Zebra set aside her menu.

"Happened," said Alice.

"Or a creep."

"Happened," said Alice.

"Or a serial killer," said Zeba.

"Might have happened. One did say he murdered someone but didn't give the number of bodies, so not sure if he was a serial or not."

"I must've missed that one," Zeba said. "How did you get out of seeing him again? I imagine you had to let him down easily."

"I told him we didn't have anything in common. I read about murder; I don't perform them." Alice continued, "There were also a couple of bored college students having fun on a school night contact me."

"You never told me about that one," Simon said.

"Didn't turn out too bad either." She drummed her splayed fingers on her cheek in memory.

"Mom?"

"We met. We had a good laugh about it. Turned out, I went bar hopping with them. Good kids." Alice straightened her back, placing her hand on her lap.

"Getting back to what I am trying to say, ReconnectNow.com, IRememberYou.com, and Letsfallinloveonemoretime.com are all different. They are about your past. There are many hidden pockets in your love cycle."

"Did you just say, 'love cycle'? And, I suppose, you want to turn those pockets inside out."

"Yes, but with a journalistic perspective. You lead this single woman, over-fifty-life that others want to experience vicariously. Let's give those lovely, over-fifty female and up through baby boomers something to dream about. It might even prod them to go on their own private journey into the past. A podcast does that."

"Podcast?"

"We lead with my monthly podcast. Tell our listeners why we are going on hiatus."

"You don't want them to be lonely forever do you, Mom?" Zeba's lips twisted into a pout.

"You can help others find love by your example."

"So now I'm a matchmaker or a failed example?"

Simon withdrew a small white flower from the vase on the table. "Their scent is lovely. This is for you.

A token of our long relationship." The tone of his voice seemed passionate. It was obvious he crafted it to gain favors but the word 'relationship' stung. She'd get him for that comment sometime but in a humorous manner.

Alice accepted the flower and tipped it to her nose. "What a nice gesture, Simon, thanks. I am not a writer like you, but if I were, this is how I'd write this scene between us: 'She smiled, pleased by his attention, feeling her face bloom like a blood moon holding a crimson secret. Feeling a bit sultry, she tucked the flower stem behind her ear as she leaned naked back in bed, had her body filled with yearning.'"

Simon coughed and downed the refilled glass of water.

Thinking she'd at least should've garnished a chuckle from Simon, Alice's throat tightened at his discomfort. No. No chance in hell would she ever hope for something more from him. Her heart couldn't risk it. Not again. Not at her age. Friendship was all Simon had to offer and she'd gladly take it. Besides, Zeba sat at her elbow also with a look of horror in protest of the verbal imagery.

"Yuck, Mother. That's just too awful."

"Zeba. I am not just your mother. I am also an entrepreneur. A friend to Simon. And a sexual being."

"Please, no more."

Simon leaned forward. "Leave the writing to me. In the meantime, let's visit some of your past sweethearts. Of course, I'll have my camera and recorder. I promise to be as unobtrusive as possible while you 'reconnect' in person."

"Let me get this straight. You want to watch my past relationships and I talk about what went wrong?"

Anger flashed.

"Not exactly like that. But sort of." Simon seemed puzzled.

"What fun! Say 'yes,' Mom. You did say you were more than my mom. Let me get to know the real you."

"Enough sarcasm, Zeba. You said 'fun'? Doesn't sound like it for me." Humiliated, Alice shook her head. The last thing she wanted was Simon at her side jotting notes when she faced her past. That part of her life was private, and she wasn't about to let Simon, nor America, see it. Online dating for safety was one matter when presented comically, but to unearth her painful past was altogether horrifying.

"You could actually rediscover love'." He raised his eyebrows. "The one man who is the true love of your life."

"I already have. Once."

"Twice." Simon corrected.

"Twice?" Zeba seemed confused.

"Ah, that's right. I keep forgetting about him." She cast an angry look at Simon who let her secret out to Zeba.

"Who is 'him'?" Zeba narrowed her eyes.

"My first husband."

"Daddy?"

"No, your dad was my second husband."

"You were married before daddy? You never told me. Are there siblings too?"

Chapter 7

"Alice, your life has been ripe with love," Simon said.

"Eww. Please don't use that word around me about Mom."

Alice corrected, "Overripe. And no, Zeba, you are still the only child. No siblings."

"Thank god."

"Your inheritance is safe."

"Great. A small oft apartment over a shabby shop and overdue credit card bills are all mine." Zeba rolled her eyes.

"Zeba, that is no way to speak to your mom."

"Your dad might be another story," Alice glibly said.

Simon cut in, "Back to the trip, shall we? Alice, it's time to see what your exes' lives have become—what yours could have been with them—good, or bad?"

"Disastrous, or catastrophic?" Alice wondered aloud.

"What a wonderful human-interest story this would be, think about it. People want to visit their past to find out what might have been. My readers like you. Know you. They trust you."

"Correction. They trust Blanche. Alice is another story."

"You're already in touch with these men online.

This will be the icing. After this, no more faux dating. You will be off the hook."

"What my life might have been with any of these men is anyone's guess and it will end up a fictional story, which probably will hack off a bunch of present wives."

Simon pulled a small notebook from his pocket along with a thin Sharpie. "We can advertise online on social media."

"Bad news. I'm banned from social media." Alice crossed her fingers under the table. "Sorry."

"What did you do this time, Mom?" Zeba rolled her eyes.

"Who gets banned from social media?" Simon shrugged.

"Me."

Simon shook his head. "I shouldn't be surprised. How many times?

"Not many."

"Five," Zeba answered. "For what this time?"

"I did something stupid. It involved a comment that wasn't well received. I seem to never learn. This time I banned myself, so I got back online this morning. I had to in order to online date for Simon. Anyway, connecting to the internet is one thing. Seeing a past love interest in person is altogether another." Alice shivered with dread. "And then a follow-up podcast too? Are you kidding me?"

Simon popped the cap off the Sharpie. "What are your past loves names?"

"You think you know me so well, Simon. But there are experiences that neither you nor Zeba know about. They are my private memories. I won't lay them out to either of you, and certainly not for public consumption. You have my internet dating-capades. But real past loves—no." Alice heaved a heavy sigh. Just a moment ago Simon suggested a getaway with just the two of them, and now, it seemed he invited a boatload of men.

"That many?" Zeba pouted.

"Go easy on your mom, Zeba—she grew up during the Age of Aquarius."

Alice sat straighter, folded her hands into her lap, and took a deep breath. "Married. Divorced. Oh, how I envy women who can say they were widowed. It seems more acceptable, free from any moral judgement. He dies. No one is at fault!"

"Unless it's murder."

Zeba pulled out an iPad from her purse. "What's his name? Your first husband's name?"

"Shut that thing off. No. I won't have you search for him."

"Mom, just let me have a look. Do this for me?"

Alice caved and told her.

"I found him. He lives about ten hours away. He remarried. Look." Zeba passed her mom her iPad.

"No thanks." Alice pushed it away.

"Okay. I can see that one upsets you, even more than Dad. So, I'll let that one go—for now."

"I feel like I'm being interrogated. I always give away more information than I intend. This time I won't."

"Mom."

"Alice."

No way would she ever want to be privy to Simon's conquests, but then again, she had a displaced romantic soft spot for him, which ebbed and flowed from time to time, and never entirely dried up. She looked from face to face. They both stared at her with pleading eyes. She felt her resolve weaken. This was never good; any moment now, Alice knew she'd give in.

"Oh, all right. But, if you're going to write them down, you'll need these." Alice pulled a handful of napkins from the dispenser. She plopped them on the table. "I'll go slowly so you have time to write. Let me see, there is Scott, Jon spelled without an h, and John spelled with an h, Rusty, David, Jack, Bob, Ross, Tom, Joel, Ralph, Stan, Steve, Jack, and…Sam. That is all I am telling." Adding the last sentence gave her a sense of regaining a bit of power. By the scowl on his face, Alice could tell Simon silently judged her.

"That many?" Zeba printed each letter in caps. One name per napkin.

"These are the ones I'm in touch with. That's what you wanted, right, Simon?"

"More napkins, please, waitress," Zeba called with her hand raised.

"I had no idea there were so many," he gasped.

"See? There are too many for one summer." Still feeling warm, Alice grabbed the napkins and cooled herself by fanning herself with them. "Simon, you'll have to find someone with less of a history to work with. I may know someone I can recommend."

"It's you I want. You are so colorful, Alice. Funny. Adventuresome. Compassionate. It's your story that sells. People know you."

The waitress traded the empty napkin holder for one already filled.

"Thanks." Simon acknowledged.

"Blanche," she corrected. "I already told you. They know Blanche." She had been sitting too long. Her lower back ached, and she needed to walk a bit to loosen the stiffness in her legs. She pushed the bill toward Simon, then noticed her glasses were still on the table and returned them to her purse, signaling her desire to leave. But seconds passed before anyone moved or spoke. "Can't either of you read body language? I'm ready to go."

"Not so fast. Which names are the most important for you to visit?" Simon asked.

Alice felt a wave of disappointment. "Simon, I have a life right here. It's a good solid life. I'm not the same person these men once knew—not physically, mentally, or emotionally. Besides, Zeba and I have her wedding to plan. There's my shop. And recently I've been commissioned to do a baby's room for twin girls."

"Whose twins?" Simon asked.

"Talia and Luis Arroyo's."

"I can take up the slack at the shop and do the baby room. I grew up helping in the shop. I know your design tastes. Mom, you'll only be gone a few weeks."

"A month at the most," Simon said. "The summer at the longest."

"Simon, are your fingers crossed in a lie under the table?"

"We already have my wedding dress, Mom."

"There's more to getting married than just the dress."

"You'd be the one to know, with all your husbands." Zeba crossed her arms.

"I'll ignore that comment for now." Alice counted on her fingers. "There's picking the invitations and the lettering and deciding on the phraseology. There is the dinner menu to be chosen, guest list, the place cards—who sits where. Figure out who the flower girl will be and the ring bearer too. How many bridesmaids, Zeba?"

"Give me a deadline."

"One week."

"Only a week?" Zeba whined.

"Then we are going?" Simon brightened. "We're leaving next week?"

"Mom, I've worked alongside you for years on home design. Give me the plans and I will follow through."

"Please," Simon begged.

Zeba grabbed the napkins back from her mother. "Okay, if these are too many, pick three men you want to see. Just like the lotto, Pick three. Revisit love and passion, for the sake of bell bottoms and Woodstock."

Alice bit her lip in a smile. "Only three? That's too hard."

"Okay, then I'll pick! How about Jack?" Zeba held out his napkin.

Alice snatched it before crumpling it into a ball. She vehemently shook her head.

"Okay, I take that as a 'no'," Simon said, tucking the napkin into his pocket. "But your reaction to this Jack makes me curious. Let's not be so hasty to dismiss him."

"That reaction makes me curious, too," Zeba said. "I want to know more."

Simon stared at her as though trying to figure her out.

"Pick the three you have unfinished business with."

"Okay. Zeba. Simon. I do not choose Jack. He lives

42

in Illinois," Alice answered almost too quickly. "I choose Andy."

"Andy?" Simon and Zeba chimed at once.

"He's not even in the mix," Simon said.

"He is now. Zeba, write down his name."

"One down, two to go," Simon prodded enthusiastically.

"For number two, John with an h. He's still in Wisconsin."

Zeba placed that napkin on top of the first one.

Several minutes passed while Alice fixated on the remaining names. She settled back into the booth and hesitated, trying to decide. Welled-up tears clouded her eyes.

"Are you okay?"

Alice shook herself out of her daydream. "If we do this, then I want to visit my parents too. It's been a while. They are about to celebrate their sixtieth anniversary."

"If there are any remaining men in your past living in the area, let's invite them too."

"Are you sure, Mom?"

She nodded. "It's time."

"It'll be a party."

"Yes, we will visit your parents."

"Thanks, Simon." She patted his hand. He threaded his fingers through hers.

"I've known you all this time and never met them." He gave her fingers a squeeze.

"Brace yourself," Zeba said.

"Maybe we can put them on the podcast too." Simon added the last name to his notebook.

"Wait. I thought I was the star?" Alice protested

with sarcasm. "You are getting ahead of yourself. I still haven't agreed." Alice tapped Zeba's shoulder and waved her down the booth.

Alice held the corner of the table to stand and then nonchalantly stretched her legs, pretending to be occupied with searching through her purse for something. Her hand brushed against chewing gum which she unwrapped and slid into her mouth. She didn't want her daughter, or Simon, to know how painful her arthritis had gotten in the past month. "It's time I get my new inventory cleaned, marked, and onto the floor. Gotta go. I need to get ready for Billy Beau, the snake charmer. My next date in a few hours. He can't wait to meet Blanche."

"Alice, I will give you my entire advance and half the profits from the book sales," Simon pleaded.

"Book? What book? Sales?" Alice grew livid. "We have gone from a nice, fun dating column that pays your bills, not mine, as you wait for another big break in serious journalism."

"I have always offered you money,"

"Now we talk podcasts, with past boyfriends and why we didn't work out. It's embarrassing."

"Sounds exciting to me. How about you, Zeba?" Simon asked.

"Definitely."

"And book too! This is way too much. Are you serious?" Alice was 'taken aback. What was the motive behind his generosity?

"I am quite serious. My agent made this deal for me. I took it. Found out about it just as I drove back from NOLA."

"Ah, the reason for the phone call. I thought you

missed me." She lifted her shoulders.

"I did miss you but this is important to me, and I know purchasing a house for you is important. It'll allow you to do that. Let me do this for you. A trade. Your history in a book for me to raise my public visibility and for you, a home."

"Do this for *me*? You are doing it for yourself. It sounds like you already wrote the proposal and received the advance." Alice felt her face burning. "You are desperate, aren't you?"

"You are correct but only partially. I want you to see this as an opportunity. After being approached for us to do a podcast all about you, on a whim, I sent the book proposal to my agent who sent it to a publisher, expecting it to be turned down along with the other pitches." Simon nervously laughed. "You can only imagine how surprised I was to get it approved."

"When was the contract signed?" Alice snapped.

He pulled it from his jeans pocket and handed it to her.

Alice grabbed it. She read, puffing out a sigh of relief. "You haven't signed it yet."

"No."

"Wow! That is a staggering amount of money they've offered you."

"It's yours. I will give it all to you. It could be our break."

"Your break. My home." Alice pushed open the café door and was immediately hit with the heat of Texas hell plus humidity.

"Alice."

"Mom."

"Give me time. When I've decided I'll call you."

Alice made a noncommittal humming sound. "I still have one more name to pick."

"Just don't wait too long. My last article on "The Importance of Water in Small Town Dating," bombed. Until my career is out of the toilet, I hope no one flushes."

Chapter 8

Talia Arroyo

The Hispanic woman sat on the couch and watched the street for Alice's car. She rubbed her round belly. With two babies growing inside, sleep was nearly elusive in her seventh month. Looking forward to delivery, she also wanted them to stay put until full term.

Not given to forming new friendships easily, Talia surprised herself when she gravitated toward forming a bond with Alice. The woman had spunk and a warm personality—as well as a distinctive eye in design. They met in Alice's shop shortly after Talia arrived home from Paris.

Alice sat at the back of the store, wrangling an old light fixture, making it into something more modern with older objects, while glimpsing at her cell. Somehow the kitchen implements that were drilled and wired and then fitted with amazing halogen lights worked. She insisted Alice turn out the store lights so she could see it light. It was magic. It was the first purchase of many that followed.

Despite the age difference, the women immediately became great friends and met for lunch a few times a month. To her own amazement, Talia even handed over the redesign of her master bedroom to Alice, rather than do it herself. Once she saw how the woman was able to keep the original charm while incorporating modern conveniences, she knew there was only one designer who could adequately capture the fairy-tale charm she envisioned for her twin girls' room.

The doorbell rang. Alice breezed through the front door, loaded with ideas, large swatches, and paint samples. Zeba followed. She toted boxes of illustrations up the steps to the second-floor bedroom with bay windows.

Talia eased down into an overstuffed chair and watched as the women measured the floor, walls, and windows. Alice listened intently, taking notes, as Talia talked about her vision. Within the hour, the paint, rugs, furnishings, and pictures had been chosen. "And I have a surprise that will be the centerpiece of the room."

"What?" Talia excitedly asked.

"As I said, it's a surprise," Alice laughed. "Patience."

Zeba left while the other women went to the kitchen to drink hot tea and devour the freshly baked sopapillas.

"You look preoccupied, my friend." Talia wiped the honey drips from the marble counter.

"I'm. Sorry. Yesterday, Simon and I had lunch."

"How is Simon?"

"Good. The reason for the lunch, he wanted to run a new idea by me. It's more like a rerun of an old idea but in a new context." Alice's finger drew invisible circles in the air.

"Tell me." Talia was totally interested. She enjoyed creative people.

"He wants to do a book on past relationships.

Mine." Alice's words seemed scripted and were followed with phrases; "I have work responsibility. There's Zeba's wedding."

"You feel uncomfortable about this?" Talia treaded carefully, not wanting to push.

"Very. So many implications." Alice raised an eyebrow. I picture myself in a humiliating situation. I'm not twenty anymore. Not forty either. And several years over fifty."

Talia reached across the counter to her friend, searching to find the words to say. Alice needed to realize the exquisite lady she had transformed into over the years. "The years have been good to you. Not only are you a beautiful woman with character in your face and in your soul. But you are living a good life. You raised a daughter on your own and educated her. Goodness, let's not forget you own a popular business."

"A struggling, business," Alice corrected, licking the honey from the tips of her fingers.

"I didn't realize you're struggling." That statement caught Talia off guard.

"Things aren't so bad. I make ends meet. Barely. I just am not in a place I can rest on my laurels. Not yet, if ever. Women my age at least have a home of their own. Not me. I still live in this little hovel above a shop."

"It's an adorable hovel and an amazing shop of curiosities."

"Thanks."

"Maybe there is something more you are feeling." Talia tried to evaluate the cause of Alice's reluctance. "Do you feel tip-toeing into your past might be a huge mistake?"

"Tip-toeing might be okay, but we are talking about an entire book—with pictures. Tip-toeing you say. It's more like a marathon race finished with a plunge off a cliff—followed by what might be public and private humiliation."

"That bad, huh?"

Alice sighed. "It's impossible to undo mistakes. Once you make one, it's yours. It can't be returned to a store. Or tossed out with the trash. Cannot be erased like a chalkboard. It stays in your heart and memory. The terrible secrets you carry become heavy to carry."

Talia searched for words to comfort her friend and reached for her hand. "Everyone has regrets."

Alice squeezed Talia's hand, blinking back tears. "What will Zeba think? My parents? My customers?"

"They will think you were young and immature—just as they once were."

"Not that young. I was at the age of 'I should have known better by now.'"

"Well, then, since that's the case, the book will be a bestseller."

"There will be public opinion of me. But—"

"But?" She held up the platter and Alice helped herself to another tasty dessert.

"I've been offered a nice amount of money." Alice coyly smiled.

"Then it's tempting."

"Talia." Tears welled as she placed her hand over her heart. "I can buy a house. My house. A small house, but a real home. Large windows, perhaps a wall with exposed brick, old wood floors with pegs—if the book does well, even more."

"Sounds lovely. But public opinion holds you

back?" Talia watched Alice's eyes close. "I have an idea. Let's see what people think of you now."

"What?"

Talia set her laptop on the counter. "I am googling Simon's column page. When I read his stories about you, I only see positive remarks."

"Really?" Alice looked surprised.

"Don't you read them?" Now Talia felt surprised.

"Sometimes. Not often. I don't want to feel as though I am pandering to please the readers. I want to be pure in my dating experiences."

"Ah, here is the latest." Shocked, she continued, "Oh my, you were groped beneath the table by a man who sat beside you?"

"Yes. He said no one would notice because of the napkin on my lap."

"What balls."

"I noticed. And shoved his hand away. I told him I needed the restroom, which I did so I could vomit. Instead, I wound up in the kitchen looking for a door outside. When I told the chef what happened, he helped me out the window."

Talia had been reading the column while listening to Alice. "You took the bus home, leaving your car."

"Actually, I got a lift from a stranger getting into his car. He was a gentleman and took me right home. Well, actually he took me to the home he thought was mine. But I live just blocks away from where I had him drop me. I thought saying a bus would be a better scenario for my reader, so they didn't feel alarmed over my real route of escape. And I didn't want my icky date to notice me peeling out of the parking lot via my car. I needed a clean getaway and picked up my car the following day."

"Why didn't you just smack the man and walk out?" Talia wondered out loud.

"Because I don't like scenes. And it was impossible to get up. He had me hemmed in, sitting right beside me in the booth. I had to excuse myself for the restroom and just kept going."

"Let me read from the blog. Here is the first comment: '*I was raised to always be polite and put up with rudeness. You help me know what not to put up with. How did you get so brave? Thanks.*'

"Here's another: '*There are no road maps to dating. But there is this column. Alice is the kind of person I would love to have as a friend.*'"

"Really? Someone said that? Let me see." Alice turned the computer to read.

"Yes, and there are twenty more comments. Should I read them?"

"I'll read them when I get home. It makes me feel better."

"You've never done an online search to see what's out there about you?"

Alice shook her head.

"Everyone does an online search."

"I don't have time to devote to this."

"I'm searching you now."

Alice got up and read over Talia's shoulder, her head low as her eyes darted back and forth. There was Simon's column, white pages with various Alice Rigby's listed across the United States, a string of photos, a few of them belonged to her. "Those pictures are all from social networks. Wow. I must admit, I use social media quite a bit. Perhaps a bit too much. I don't like all that information out there."

"Well, you are out there on the world wide web, but only minimally in most cases. I see nothing damaging. Where are your reasons not to go now?"

"If you must know—it's my body. It's perfectly icky. I spend time at the gym every day—okay, a few times a week—okay, once or twice a month, maybe every other month, I should really say but look at me." Much to Talia's surprise, Alice lifted her blouse, revealing flesh and patted her tummy. "I jiggle." Then she pulled up her sleeves and wiggled her arms. "Look! Cafeteria lady arms. The other day I had on a short-sleeved blouse. And as I reached for something, out of the corner of my eye I saw a piece of old tissue paper. I pulled on it to get it off me. It wasn't tissue paper after all. It turned out to be my arm."

Talia laughed and winked. "It's not as bad as all that."

"I need to dress like one of those hyper-religious women with a collar up to my neck, sleeves to my wrist, and a hemline to my ankles."

"Do you know what I see? A stunning woman with lovely thick hair. You are slim and look as sexy in a skirt as you do in jeans."

"Sexy? Me? Ha."

"Not only that but you are fun to be with. Any man who ends up with you is lucky. Go. Have fun this summer. Discover yourself—the woman you are now."

"And you are forgetting a very important piece." Talia folded her napkin into fours. She spoke with earnest, "There is a baby room I need to complete."

"It seems to me we made good progress on the choices today. Stop making excuses."

"If I do decide to go, and I emphasize the word *if*, how do you feel about Zeba stepping in to oversee the project? We will talk daily, I promise. She will send me pictures of updates. If there is anything you are displeased with, I will have it fixed immediately."

Talia held both Alice's hands and looked her in the eyes. "My babies still have a few months inside of me—hopefully. Meanwhile, your daughter can take charge. There is nothing that cannot be fixed, if need be, later."

"I want this room ready and perfect long before they are born."

"The first months I plan on having them with Luis and myself in our room. He's taking time from work to be with us."

"What a sweet guy."

"I got lucky with him." Talia's heart throbbed with such force that she feared it would overpower her, consumed by the love she held for her husband.

"You will be the most wonderful mother. Did you know at the turn of the century, pink was for boys and blue was for girls?"

"No idea!" Talia clapped her hands.

Alice looked at her watch, slid off the stool, and reached for her oversized purse. "I should get going. I still need to close the shop for the day and have a big decision to make."

"Your spirit is still very much intact but it's time to free it. Throw caution to the wind. Go and find your past loves. Maybe one will step up and become your future. And if not, that's okay too, because you have not lost yourself. And if worse comes to worse, you will finally own a home, as well as the expenses that come with it."

"Thanks."

Alice stood at the door threshold. "Daylight has dropped. It's so beautiful here. I look at this town of Denton that I love so very much and miss Zeba already."

"So, you are going on this trip?"

"Perhaps. But what will become of my place here if I am not here to fill my role?"

"The shop will open every day—Stella will see to that. And she'll go to estate sales in your place. Zeba will be in constant motion to see that the baby's room finishes on time. As for me, I will continue taking my baby vitamins and get enough rest."

"And walk through the babies' room a dozen times a day wondering if you made the right selections. And all this will occur, after all of you realize no one can make final decisions without me." Alice stepped onto the top step.

"One word of caution."

Alice tilted her head.

"Out there, be careful what you search for."

Alice straightened her back. "You just gave me chills.

Chapter 9

Zeba

"Darling. You're home. Where have you been all day?" Martin stood at the stove in their apartment.

"On a mission with my mom." Zeba looked for an uncluttered spot to set the box of samples. "Dinner smells good by the way."

"Your mom? A mission? Let me take that for you." He lifted the box from her and set it on the floor against a wall. "What is this stuff?"

"Paint. Wallpaper samples. Rug samples." Zeba looked long at the dark curly-headed man she had betrothed her life to. "She's taking off for the summer with Simon."

"Wow. I never saw that coming. Good for her. So, there is romance between them after all. Yay, Alice. I'd like to see them together."

"Romance? Between them? No way. Why would you even say that?" Zeba felt annoyed about the pairing.

"Summer—together—longtime friend. I've seen the way they look at one another."

"Don't be ridiculous. He's an old friend. If something were to happen, it would have done so a long time ago."

"Then why the trip?"

"It's for a book he's writing or wanting to do about my mom. Meanwhile, it is I who will be taking over for her at the shop and guess what else?" Zeba twirled around the room.

"Tell me."

"I'm also doing Talia Davila's baby room. Well, I'll follow Mom's instructions but I have ideas of my own to incorporate."

"I hope you are being paid for this." He set the table.

"Of course, I am." Zeba frowned.

"You don't look happy about it."

"Why do you say that?" Zeba lifted the lid on the pot to see the chicken.

"Dinner. Made just the way you like. Balsamic chicken with Mediterranean salsa and broccoli with crunchy herb topping. Chocolate mousse for dessert. Just for you." He kissed her cheek and again commented, "You don't look happy."

"You can have the chicken. I'll take a salad."

"Wait—didn't you tell me this morning you wanted chicken for dinner?" Martin crossed his arms and leaned against the kitchen counter.

Zeba crossed her arms to mimic him. "I changed my mind."

"No problem." He shrugged.

Zeba quietly removed arugula and raw vegetables from the fridge. She began chopping them on the butcher block. "Decorating is something I have always wanted to do."

"I had no idea until this very moment."

"Then you do need to pay more attention. Mom doesn't trust me. I need to prove myself. So, by doing a great job for Talia, Mom will have no other choice but to take me on as a partner."

"Don't partners usually buy in?"

"Well, Mother should just give me half the business. I am her daughter."

"If that is what you want, then I hope that happens since you are her daughter and want to be given something you haven't earned."

"What? You talk to me as though I'm a child." Hoping to deflect blame, she drew in a sharp, angry breath. "Is that what you think of me?"

"Let's not have another argument about your mom. Anyway, to me, it seems as though you are trying to force your mom's hand. Remember, she runs a small business in a small town. Alice isn't about to hand it over to you—even if she is your mother."

"Do you hear how belittling you are?"

Martin pulled a portion of the chicken from the pot along with cooked vegetables to set on his plate before walking to the table.

She watched him. "My, but you are suddenly quiet. Nothing more to say?"

"Just hungry. I refuse to argue."

Zeba joined her fiancée at the table. "Today I found out something very interesting about my mother."

"Oh?"

"My mom had a sordid past with many men."

"And you just found this out today?"

"Yes, it seems Mother has secrets. Unpleasant secrets. Now I know she isn't capable of love. I wonder if she was born that way, or if a childhood tragedy made her like that."

"I say, good for her. Alice is filled with love. She shines with it, and she loves you very much. I see it."

"Loves me? Mother took me away from my dad when I was five. Then, instead of staying in the city so I could be near him, along with everyone I knew, she moved us from a large, beautiful home with a maid and a swimming pool, to a hovel of a loft, where she still resides as though she were destitute hobbit."

"Maybe she likes it. Each to his, or her own."

"Whatever." Zeba dipped a crouton into the dressing and munched on it.

"Didn't you visit your dad growing up?"

"Every vacation. It only served as a cruel reminder of what I lost. I never wanted to come back to Texas. I hate every inch of this state."

"Then why did you?"

Zeba got up and poured herself a glass of wine. She held it up. "Want one?"

"Sure."

"I never wanted to come back here. But in my absence, my dad remarried. She's okay, but something changed between Dad and me. Suddenly, I was treated as a guest, not a member of the family." Zeba brought the bottle along with a wine glass for Martin. "In some ways, I feel I never really had a home. Things changed for my dad. But everything stayed the same with Mom. She wore the same clothes, and she said the same things, and she always hauled something horrid home from the curb to clean, fix and sell. Things smelled old."

"Divorce is hard on children."

"That's not the only thing I endured because of my mother's choices. I had to endure private schools."

"And therefore, you received a great education."

Zeba bristled, feeling more and more agitated at Martin's defense of her mother. She was his fiancée, not dear Alice. "I received a great education indeed while being the designated cast away. Chauffeurs drove my peers to school until their sixteenth birthday when they were given any car they wanted. Do you know what I rode in as a kid, and what I got for my sixteenth birthday?"

"Tell me." He ran his fingers through his hair.

"Stop being so critical, will you?"

"Sorry." Martin stared at the carrots.

"As a kid, Mother picked me up and dropped me off from school. At the time, we had some two-door rattletrap that was about ten years old. It was usually crammed full of old furniture in disrepair, parked in the middle of a line of sleek black limos, humiliating me. For my sixteenth birthday, she bought insurance so I could drive that car."

Martin let out a small laugh.

"You find that funny?" It felt like he was patronizing her. She grew livid.

"No, it's just the way it was said. Sorry, again. Continue."

"I called Dad." She emptied her glass and set it back on the table before pouring another, proud of what happened as a result.

"Don't tell me. By doing so, you got the car you wanted."

"I got the car I deserved. Dad loves me."

"Love has nothing to do with gifts." Martin pushed back his unfinished dinner. "Guess I am not as hungry as I thought."

"You seem mad I got my car."

Martin crossed his arms over his chest. "Parents should agree. It seems you got in between them—made it worse."

"They were divorced, Martin." Zeba seethed. "I shamed her. Dad shamed her. From then on, I got what I wanted."

"And yet you still lived in the loft."

"True. But things changed when I went to college. I got a lovely apartment. Mother paid for it."

"Your mother constantly struggled. Why not your dad?"

"I told Mother that I would ask Dad to pay for a nice apartment, not the unlivable loft we stayed in. She got out her checkbook and paid for what I wanted."

"You do seem to get your way." He sighed, standing to his feet in order to clear the table.

"Exactly. I know my way around my mother. Just watch. I'll run that shop of hers in no time at all." Now she stood. "And make money at it too."

"I have full confidence in your abilities to manipulate."

Zeba huffed as she got up from the table and threw her napkin down.

Chapter 10

Date Night—Texas Rifle Restaurant

Alice felt pretty in red embellished ankle jeans and a detailed button-down blouse. Large hand-stamped sterling Navajo earrings adorned her ears with her hair billowing out over her shoulders. Lastly, the turquoise bracelet and ring were the perfect touch. If only Simon could see her right now. She looked and felt pretty. Confidence oozed. And then Billy appeared with worn jeans and a cowboy snapped shirt. Well, at least he looked showered and wore a shirt that wasn't stained.

"Hey, there. You sure look prettier than your picture, Blanche."

"Thank you, Billy," she greeted as he slid in beside her, his thigh touching hers.

The ballsy move made her ill at ease. The newbie man putting his frame so close in proximity to hers, it was totally out of the realm of acceptable etiquette. What if he whipped out a snake from his pocket, or a fleshy one out from his pants? She shivered. And not in a good way.

"I'd be able to see you better if you moved to the other side of the table." She pointed the way.

"I have a problem." It was his turn to point and he pointed to the hearing aid in his left ear. "Best I stay here so we can have a conversation."

His hand worked its way to her knee.

"Move your hand. Sit over there." Now she pointed to the table next to them.

"You want me to sit at another table?"

"Please." She batted her false eyelashes at him.

He got up and left.

"Psst. There goes that story." Alice ordered a medium rare rib eye and salad with blue cheese on the side.

****

Two days later—Alice

A halo of sallow light from a small table lamp fell about the tiny room. Just enough brightness to find her way.

Dressed in a cotton nightgown, she took a long sip of iced tea while booting her computer. Its hum felt comforting. The screen flashed and, in nanoseconds, a message from Jack appeared. If she had any sense, she wouldn't read the instant message. Refused to read it. Closed her computer lid and walked around the small room taking long deep breaths. Looking in the fridge she decided on the apple for her snack. She cut it into slices and dribbled honey on it.

Then she hurried across the room, forgetting all about the apple, and opened the computer lid. Okay, she'd read it. *Let's face it, if I had any sense long ago, I never would have reconnected with him—not now and certainly not then.* Yet, hearing from Jack proved to be rather satisfying in a redemptive sort of way. But now, at this moment, she had a plan to set everything right again. Yes, she grew fickle.

—*Are you there, Texas?*—

—*Hello, Illinois Jack. I am now.*— Chatting on

messenger made her feel flirty and wicked in a puritanical manner. She was safely tucked in bed with a sheet over her, and in her imagination, she was sixteen—okay, maybe twenty-three. It wasn't the screen she really saw anymore, but his face in her memory. Dead feelings reawakened. When he stopped calling, it took two years to feel normal again, so why was she opening the door again, even if it was just a small crack? For a moment, she gloated over the fact that he was talking to her again, after so long.

—Hello, Texas Alice. How'd you get so far away from me?— Suddenly, his face came up filling the screen. His dark hair now threaded with white. Large blue eyes. A cocky feel good smile showing all his teeth. She drew back knowing her face didn't have a bit of makeup and her hair was half up and half down.

"What did you just do?" She held a bedsheet up to her chin.

"It's called Facetime." He scrunched his face good-naturedly.

"I know what it's called but I needed a warning. I am not ready to be seen."

"You sure look good to me." He licked his lips.

He sure looked good to her too but wasn't about to say that.

"So, why Texas?"

"To answer your first question, I got this far because we lost contact." Her heart leaped up in her chest.

"Your words wound me."

"Truth can do that. Hey, did you get my picture? I emailed it last night. But here I am in all my natural beauty." Alice rolled her eyes and held the sheet tighter as she waited for his response.

"I did. You look better in person."

The flood of relief was immediate.

"I want to see you again. It's been a long time since our last kiss. Too long."

"Do you remember where that took place?" She raised an eyebrow. It was a test of sorts.

"We stood on Monroe Street, right across from Lake Michigan, the five-star hotel behind us. It was a cold afternoon, and I was trying to warm you up. I hope I did a good job."

Her eyes misted. Alice fell back into her pillows, amazed at Jack's spot-on memory. After all, since the day they walked in opposite directions, there must have been hundreds of women that stormed through his life—okay not hundreds, but most likely dozens—many, many dozens. Married or single, it never mattered. She sat back up.

"There you are," Jack said. "I wondered where you went. Perhaps we should meet again. Same spot? Unless you remarried? Engaged? It doesn't really matter."

"Maybe not a good idea."

"Please say you are going to be in Illinois. We can reenact our last day together."

"No, no, no."

"Why not?"

"Afterward, you will tell me the same thing you said the last time we were together." A gush of sentiment labeled THE PAST lightening through her cells. This guy conjured up such emotion. Did it hurt? Anger? Disappointment? Unrequited love? What this leftover feeling anyway?

"Alice. Alice. Alice. I want to see you. Hold you. Come to Illinois. I will tell you anything you want."

"The truth."

"The truth."

"What stays in my mind is when we said our goodbyes and you gave me a push through the airport doors to be rid of me. I might be in touch. Until then, happy trails." She stared at the screen, empowered by cutting off the conversation first. No, she wouldn't see Jack. Mistake number three. Never again.

Another computer ding. This one from Sam, who wasn't even on her list, but the one person she'd love to see the most. A text from Sam sent hours ago. Had she made a mistake in who she wanted to visit when she gave Zeba the names? She could switch some of them around like a veritable game of checkers. She did have a number three to pick out. And she could easily plus it.

If so, she'd never trade Sam. Like the others, they rediscovered one another online. But, with him, there was no flaming emotion attached. It was a sweet relationship she didn't want to relinquish. And there was clearly no reason to. The long-ago sweet romance had now turned into a wintertime friendship. Satisfying. Right then she needed to talk. But it was late. He might have gone to sleep.

—*Sam.*—she typed.

—*Alice. I was hoping to hear from you tonight.*—

—*Bad day?*—

—*Better now. Hey, there's something I want to tell you.*—

—*Tell me.*—

—*I've had time to look back on my life*—

—*I imagine, but don't*—

—Especially our time together.—

—It was a sweet time in our lives. Both of us innocent.—

—I remember your essence. Naive. Trusting. Sweet.—

—You're making me smile, Sam.—

—Then I've done my job. Alice, listen to me, you need to find a good man. No settling. Someone who will treat you like a queen. You're deserving.—

Tears ran down her cheeks and fell onto the keyboard. She wiped her nose on the sleeve of her nightgown.

*—I just want to say, I'm sorry for back then.—*he texted.

*—It's okay. And I am sorry about now.—*she texted back.

Long silence. No printed words crossed the screen. She waited.

—Sam?—

—Still here.—

—What if I came to see you?—

—Really? When?—

—Soon.—

—I'd like that.—

—I'll take a road trip. To see you. I will let you know when I am a few days out.—

—Don't put it off. Okay? You know why.—

—I do. Till then.—

—I love you, Alice.—

*—I love you, Sam. Say hi to Claire for me.—*Her heart felt as if it were at the base of her throat, heavy and hurting. There were all types of love. She closed the lid on her computer, hugging it against her. Maybe

Simon was right. Maybe it was time to find out what life could have been had she picked differently. Maybe she should take a step forward to meet her past in the present. She just might find her future there. No more performing life analysis, for she would have all the answers when she returned home at the end of the summer, especially about Simon.

Alice looked around at the walls of her small space. Everything she owned was practically within arm's reach. How did she and Zeba ever manage in this space together for such a long time? She dreamed of a vintage house on a quaint tree-lined sweet. Historic District? Expensive but where she wanted to be. One story. No steps. Space for her projects. The ability to acquire more material goods than just her needs. All these years, one would think she'd have more to show. Maybe a peek into her past would be the answer to home ownership.

However, she had spent her money well. Zeba never lacked for anything, and was handed the best private education, dressed well, went on vacations, went to college, and graduated without debts.

She achieved all of this because she worked long hours at the shop for years and provided Simon with feedback on the dates she sometimes suffered through for his column. At times, she accepted payment for these stories because she needed it, and he insisted. However, it made her feel callous to date for a rate. Honor was important. Alice genuinely felt interested in finding someone smart and kind. Sharing her stories with Simon also kept him close—and it was fun reading them online. A veritable diary of her life. Maybe this was a sign. She could venture out to see what happens.

It'd be better than more snake handlers who just wanted to handle her with the snake in his pants.

Okay. She'd do it.

She shifted on the pullout bed and heard the creak of the frame. It was time to decide what to pack. Peering into the closet, she decided causal was best. It was comfortable. A couple of pairs of shoes. Two bras. Socks. Nylons? Nope, no nylons. She hiked up her nightgown and took a good look at her legs under the light. Maybe she should reconsider wearing nylons. But long dresses were nice too, in style and they also hid a hell of a lot—like the scar on her left knee from surgery.

Pushing through the hanging clothes, she tried them on—not liking most. Too worn out, which translated into somehow she stopped caring how she looked, except when Simon was around. What happened to her?

Alice squared her shoulders. A new day was coming, if only she let it. No longer would she be an epic fashion disaster. If the clothes weren't good enough for her future, they sure weren't good enough for her present. She pulled worn slacks and tight shirts and piled sweaters from hangers, shoving them into garbage bags. Hands on her hips, she looked around the room. Now what?

There, on her bed, nestled in the middle of her covers, was the laptop where she left it. Online shipping might be a good option. But, if she waited until they arrived, they might not look right on her or fit like they should. No. This is something she needed to handle in person. Besides, she could have fun shopping for clothes along the way, if she could convince Simon to veer from the interstate now and then.

Alice wheeled her suitcase from the closet and started packing her favorite perfume, coconut body wash and lotion, electric toothbrush, 3-D whitening toothpaste, and drugstore makeup. Something caught her eye which also caught her breath. She had forgotten she still had it. The skirt. Not just any skirt. It was the 1970s skirt of the white gauze peasant dress, snagged on the closet latch. Did it still fit? Naked, she slipped the dress over her head. It easily slipped right on, although not with the same fullness, probably because her girth had increased—but it worked. And work even better if she located a girdle.

And then it happened. A light feeling overwhelmed her. Not only did she feel years dissolve, but she became chocked full of hope and unbridled passion. *Oh, my goodness, the dress is a magic potion!* Eagerly, Alice dug through a dresser and pulled out a ratty, cracked, dog-eared photo album. Easing down to the carpet, she sat with her legs stretched out, her back against the end of the bed, the book on her lap. Paging through, she ran her fingers over the young, motionless faces with fixed gazes. So many people, most of their names forgotten. And then there she was, smiling and looking into the camera, pinching out the skirt of the peasant dress with her fingers as she danced. A ring of white daisies crowned her head. Her breath paused. Her heart beat faster. She suddenly felt the pulse of that eighteen-year-old girl who was innocent, pure, and had not yet seen genitals—especially not hairy ones. She burst out laughing at the thought of herself having once been so rattled by it. *Life should be filled with second chances and more poems about two roads diverging in the yellow woods and forging new paths! Scott Fitzgerald was right when he wrote: There are all kinds of love in the world but never the same kind twice.*

Once upon a time, she fancied herself an artist. She could have been a teacher. Or a world-renowned artist giving shows at galleries. Is that what would have happened if she hadn't freaked out at the unexpected male organ? That day, her professor gave her a shove in another direction, and she got married without her degree, not once but twice. But when she divorced, she returned to college. Life was a series of paths. An absolute network of choices and changes.

Alice folded her peasant dress into the suitcase along with a few pairs of jeans and cotton tops. She stepped back into her nightgown and covered herself again with the bed sheet. The streetlights gave off a ginger glow which sifted through the curtains onto her wood floor. Perhaps there was a second springtime on the horizon—that is if she gave it a whirl.

She decided to take that road trip into her past with Simon in his convertible sports car, top down. No sense in waiting till morning to give Simon her answer. She'd call him now. She watched the cell light up in her hand.

"What?" he groggily answered.

"Sounds like I woke you."

"Alice."

"Hi, Simon."

"Yeah." He sounded drunk.

"How soon do you want to leave?"

"We're really doing this?"

"We are really doing this. On one condition."

"Anything."

"Zeba cannot ever know about our past. It's non-negotiable."

Chapter 11

Simon

There was a familiar, annoying melody. Trying to shake sleep, he struggled with his subconscious still focused on the nonsensical dream that held him. Eyes refused to open. His head pounded sickly, and his lips felt numb. Breath came sharply into his lungs. There was a sweet, sick taste in his mouth. *Too much damn wine*.

The annoying melody persisted. Now he knew where it was coming from. Simon reached for the cell on the bedside table. His eyes were small slivers in his head; couldn't make out the caller's face on the screen. Where did he put his glasses? Pressed talk. "What?"

He only remembered bits of the conversation but did recall it was Alice who called.

"Hi, Simon."

"Yeah?" He reached for the alarm clock, automatically placing it on his chest.

"Simon, are you awake?"

Snores.

"Simon!"

"Yeah. What time is it?" He looked at his bedside table and saw the empty space where the clock needed to be. He leaned over the bed to see if it had fallen, just as the clock rolled off his chest. The alarm started ringing. He batted it with his hand, and it silenced.

"Sorry. It's after midnight. Are you awake? Drunk? Hello? Simon? This is Alice."

"Yeah." Just as he dozed back to sleep, he heard her next words.

"How soon do you want to leave?"

"Leave? You're serious? We're really going to do this?" He rubbed his forehead to placate his throbbing head.

"Yes."

The affirmation brought him from stupor to sober.

"I can be there in twenty minutes." Fumbling with covers, he did his too-much-wine version of scrambling from bed. Limping into the bathroom, he wondered why his foot suddenly hurt. Where was that aspirin bottle? Glasses. Where were they?

Alice continued. "Whoa, hold on. I haven't slept yet, and neither have I made arrangements at the shop."

"When?" He sat on the edge of the tub, running his fingers through his hair.

"Give me a week. By then, I should also be done with the preliminary designs for Talia's babies' room. I only hope she won't mind that Zeba will be executing them."

"I don't know how to thank you, Alice." He yawned while leaning over the sink and stared at his red eyes in the cabinet mirror.

"A fat paycheck is thanks enough." Alice figured money and Simon's love was all she could ever want. If she couldn't have both, she'd settle for one. But which one if it really came down to it?

"Okay, we will leave a week from tomorrow?"

"Yes, a week from tomorrow."

"Eight in the morning?"

"Meet me on the sidewalk, outside of my shop."

"Eight in the morning. Shop. You got it." Simon breathed a sigh of relief.

"One thing more."

"Anything."

"Zeba cannot ever know about our affair. It's non-negotiable."

"Us? What do you mean 'us'?"He scrunched his face.

"See you next week."

"No, wait. You don't want me to say anything to Zeba about us? I'm not sure I know what you mean. Alice? Alice?"

She left the conversation.

"Us? Us? Us? What in the world are you talking about?" He padded around the condo barefooted, clear thinking still partially blocked by wine. He slid the door to the balcony and stepped out, looking at the busy university town. The night air smelled of warm pizza. Dozens of college kids still made time of it, way past midnight, and flooded the sidewalk and streets. Just what one would expect. He used to be a night owl and party dog until age and weight slowed him. *What was Alice doing up so late anyway? Another date?* It didn't matter, in a week they'd be on the road eating fried pies at roadside cafes and having a blast.

Simon looked down the street in the direction of where Alice lived, hoping she was lost in her lovely dreams by now. Simon still held the cell in his hand. So, she agreed to his book idea. Three love stories. *What She Left Behind* might be a good title for it too. Maybe make a picture book out of it as well. It'd be interesting to see the guys she once crushed on and even more so if there lingered any emotion. If anything started up between her and an old flame, he might step in to stop it—only to protect her. Two bad marriages were quite enough. What did she want, a third? Who was he kidding? On some level, she was his anchor, and couldn't do without her. A husband would put a stop to that.

Ah, Alice. Simon thought about Alice and how she generated her own energy. He found her seductive—a woman who didn't reveal everything. She was like a present hidden in layers of tissue paper. Alice's brilliance coupled with shyness created a woman with great observation skills. He trusted her instincts—he adored listening to her. He relished this journey and hoped she'd be in his life forever.

Simon shut the balcony door and crawled back into bed, hoping he'd be able to sleep. Something poked him in his back. Reaching around, he pulled out the clock, which, for a moment, transformed into a face— Alice's. She smiled at him from the glass reflection. Her hair was long and blond and thick—like it was when they first met. Alice had just transferred colleges. "Ah, Alice." He held the clock to his chest. She was so young and lovely. He was young and stupid. And then he jolted up in bed, instantly knowing what she meant by 'Zeba can never know about us.'

Chapter 12

Simon
37 years earlier…

It was early morning when Simon walked into the coffee shop.

The young woman beside him held her purse against her chest in an odd position, making her hard to miss. Upon a closer look, she was braless and tried to hide the fact her perky breasts were cold. Doing his best not to look at her chest, he nodded.

Then she spoke, murmuring the first word, in a lifetime of words that would follow; "Hello."

"Hello. Just got done running."

"Good for you. I ran too. All the way from my apartment for a donut."

Alice dug for money in her jeans pocket.

"Let me get it." He bought breakfast.

"Thanks. You look familiar."

That made him laugh. "I think we are in the same class."

"Oh?"

"Actually, I'm the TA in your psychology class."

"I thought you looked familiar. But you are out of context here." And then she turned and walked out the door, holding a white bag of chocolate-covered donuts.

A month passed before they bumped into one

another, again at the same donut shop. "Hey donut girl," he greeted her. "Remember me?"

"You are the runner." Alice nodded.

"This is our third time meeting like this." He noticed she was wearing a jacket today. Made him wonder if she was braless beneath it.

"Third time?"

"I think second."

Her hair was messy, like she forgot to run a brush through it before leaving the apartment. At least she remembered to add the red lipstick which lit up her face.

"Third time. The first time was art class. Two years ago." Simon ordered coffee and a sugar donut, then nodded toward an empty table where they could sit. Alice paid for her chocolate cake donut and joined him.

"You were in my class then? I must've made a big impression on you for you to remember me because I never went back to class. I dropped art and took a different class."

"I was only in your class for that one day, as the model." He smiled.

Pale pink flushed her cheeks. "Now I remember. I'd say you made a big impression on me. Up to that time I had never seen a man completely naked."

"I do have a big impression to make."

Alice blushed and started to get up.

"And now?" Simon asked as he caught her arm.

"And now, I keep secrets," she coyly answered before leaving the shop.

Months later, Wisconsin was covered in winter ice and snow. Simon needed to get out of the cold. To him, it would be just another getaway—a spring break from the winter doldrums. The girl he initially asked to vacation with him had just gotten engaged. His ego took a hit. The neighborhood bar was a good place to lick his wounds.

It was after ten at night when he was bartending and high-fived a few friends who walked in, ordering a brewski. After downing several beers himself, he started toward the back to find the restroom.

And there was Alice in her loose, faded jeans, wearing a suede jacket, looking like an ingénue, chatting up a storm with a crew of girls while tucking her hair behind her ears. As he walked closer, he heard her discuss sofa covers passionately. "Gilded antique mirrors totally transform entire rooms." Who said things quirky like that? She was funny. Unexpected. Like, who cared? Only Alice.

There were other women he noticed that night, but only Alice wore funny shoes that looked like gunboats and didn't seem like she belonged in a rowdy bar. She just randomly walked around the room, stopping to speak to someone for a bit then moved around more. She also wasn't aggressive about picking up a guy.

Simon found that attractive.

Scooping up what was left of his deflated courage, he walked to her, holding up a beer that he offered. "There's the donut girl."

"And there is the TA. You know, you never talked to me in class." She playfully squinted her eyes. "I waited for you to ask me out, but you chose someone else."

"Shame on me. I just clocked out. Let's find a seat." Simon found a back booth where they spent hours talking. He found her smart and quick-witted. It

79

was as if they were the only two in that bar. Just as the place closed, he asked her to go with him to Corpus Christi. She rolled her eyes in thought and then blurted, "Yes!" It was a done deal. Maybe the snow and sub-zero climate had something to do with her quick decision.

It never occurred to him that things would be different this time, with this girl. But her attitude was clear, and innocent, without an agenda. She was trusting and open, which he found refreshing, and later realized it was because no one had ever dumped her—no broken heart to deal with. Not by then anyway. He shrugged it off. After a few days and nights in his car, and a couple of small town stops along the way, they arrived in south Texas. A motel waited. Same motel. Same room. New girl.

After a shower and a nice dinner along the shore, where they played footsy under the table, they went back to the motel. He lit candles in the dark room, as light from the moon spilled through the slight part of the curtains.

Alice stood in front of the mirror looking at herself and watching Simon walk up behind. Slowly, she tipped her head to the side and pulled her blonde hair free of the ponytail. Her curls pooled onto her shoulders and fell over her small breasts, down over her stomach, stopping just before her waist. He kissed her neck where there were small wisps of hair. He tasted the sweetness of her skin.

His small frisky neck kisses grew into deeply passionate smooches on her mouth. Hungrily he unbuttoned her blouse to see her breasts, cupped in an ordinary bra, appearing like soft, pink ripe grapefruit ready to be sucked. She seemed uncomfortable.

"Is this okay with you? We don't have to do this." Simon took a step back not wanting to force anything if she wasn't ready.

"I do want this. I want you." She nodded and bashfully pulled him to bed, where she slid under the covers. "I'm ready but shy."

"Alice, you shouldn't be. You are the most beautiful girl I've ever seen." It wasn't a lie. Suddenly, he wanted her more than he had any woman. He turned out the light and then went slow, giving her time to change her mind, hoping she wouldn't. Each gentle touch was meant for arousal. Kisses were long and intense followed by short, quick lip nibbles. When she was heavy with desire, he slowly entered the passage through her thick dark hair, entering her gently. And then, he knew her. No way he could help but look into her lovely eyes, seeing the dimensions of how she felt in that moment when he felt her contracting. Large green eyes blinked back, sparkling with tears that spoke of pain, passion, and ultimate pleasure. There was also a silent promise to love him forever. *Love? Oh no. This must be her first time.* And she was his number, what? Well, he hadn't exactly kept track.

Lost in her scent, her disappearing innocence, her unintelligible utterances, her deep desire for him—his deep desire for her—he came—hard and strong. The all-consuming orgasm was so intense he thought it would devour him, leaving nothing behind but a used condom. Clearly, it was the best sexual experience he ever imagined. Not only had she given him her body, but she had given him her adoration, and everything she was and ever would be. Until then, he didn't know how sex was meant to feel. It took him in sexually, physically, and spiritually. Afterward, they lay together without covers and void of words. When he turned to hold her, tears were draining from her eyes. Not from the pain a bursting cherry causes, but because she loved what she had experienced; how he, Simon Davenport, made her feel. For a week they made love, rarely leaving the room. As he taught her about her body, she seemed eager to learn and just as eager to please him. At those times he wanted to fall in love with her, too.

Once they were back on campus, it was as though a switch flipped. The intensity of the relationship scared him. He wasn't ready for it and certainly not ready for Alice.

Chapter 13

Excuses to break dates were plenty. He liked his life the way it was—carefree. He liked having his own place, with one key for the lock, his own computer, his own bed. He didn't want to risk losing any of it. In a few months, he graduated and took off after delivering the friendship speech to her. "We will always be friends. I will call ya sometime."

He remembered how she looked in the spring sunshine, wearing a pink flowered sundress, her face pale like wheat."I have a job offer in New York with a top magazine."

"What a great opportunity." She choked tears as though knowing he wasn't asking her to come along.

"I'm taking it." A nervous laugh escaped him.

"You should. It'd be silly not to." Her voice trailed and she looked down.

"I have two days to get out there. So, my car is packed. I'm ready to take off. I'll give you a call when I get there," he said, not altogether kindly.

She nodded and bit the nail of her left pinky.

He shrugged.

Alice became emotional. To look at her—he didn't catch it right away. It's when he held her close to him that he felt the slight quiver of distress—noticed the tears gathering in the corner of her exquisite eyes. Then she stepped back and, in an instant, looked quite put together.

He didn't kiss her and offered no apology for leaving her standing there alone. This was the trade. Freedom meant a broken heart. Running away instead of being brave enough to stay and love her. Simon wasn't up for more guilt. As an afterthought, he repeated his final words, this time over his shoulder. "I'll call."

Alice became smaller and smaller in the rearview mirror until she had entirely disappeared. Once on the interstate, a sense of relief spilled over him causing him to nearly hyperventilate. City life suited him just fine. With a laser focus on his career, he avoided the distraction of women. It paid off. A rental apartment in Brooklyn suited him just fine. Each morning he rode the subway into Manhattan, drank coffee in a small office with a big view, and the stories flowed from his fingers onto the typewriter.

Six months later, Alice came to mind. Maybe give her a holler? The call of warm sandy beaches came to mind while experiencing his first New York blizzard. The story he had worked on for the last several months came out to rave reviews and he needed to share it with someone. Maybe Alice.

After several shots of whiskey, he went back to his apartment and picked up the phone, amazed to remember the number. She just returned from a family Christmas Eve service. What a relief to hear the enthusiasm she exuded. "Simon, I couldn't be happier for you. I knew you were bound for great things. Tell me, what is your article about?"

"It's more of a story, really."

"A story," she repeated. "I love them."

"I'm on my way, Alice. I feel this is just the start."

"It is just the start of many great things coming your way. But you still haven't told me what the story is about."

He held his breath and then said the word: "You."

"What?"

He pictured her winding her finger around a blond lock of hair, puzzled over what he just said. "It's titled, *The Blonde Girl on Sandy Beaches*."

"Well, I feel honored. I want a copy. Where can I find it?"

"Any newsstand. But let me send it to you."

"Make sure it's signed. I now personally know an author. I hope you didn't use my name."

"I didn't."

"What name did you use?"

"Blanche."

"Blanche? You're kidding. What an awful name."

It was another month until they spoke again. This time, she called him, upset about a guy she had dated a few times. Together they agreed it was healthy for her to end the relationship. He couldn't recall now if she had said anything about the story. Her story.

However, they talked a lot that year. Back then, you had to pay for those long-distance phone calls. It was the most satisfying relationship he ever had—even if it was only a phone conversation with someone a thousand miles away. Then, the following New Year's Eve, she called with big news. She met someone. They were getting married. Who did that? Marry a month after meeting? Well, that didn't last. After two years, she left Charlie. And after that, came Thomas.

It was wrong from the start. Neither were in the

first blush of romance. Both in their mid to late twenties, Thomas was quiet and at first made little to no demands of her. However, he was also cold and distant. In time, life had to come on his terms, which included marriage. Alice wasn't the same gal Simon once knew—she had changed. No longer did she talk about how to transform rooms into warm living spaces or paint chips, or antique mirrors, or why original hardwood floors are so much better than carpets.

His Alice was all about the next catered dinner party and moving into a bigger house, this time with a pool. Thomas hired an interior decorator rather than trust his wife to use her talents. Alice's brain shut off and her spirit shut down. Simon missed the former Alice. This Alice was determined to make this marriage stick—even though she had to finally give up talking to Simon along with her decorating passion.

And then five years after the birth of Zeba, she decided to leave. He was the first one she called.

"I've lost myself; who I am. I am living in an unfamiliar world and can feel myself falling apart. I had dreams when I married Thomas—but now, I barely recognize myself, and my dreams are now thin as vapor, spun by a different girl."

"Alice, you sound awful."

"Simon, listen. It's not just me who is being affected, but it's tough on Zeba too. I see her spirit daily being crushed. I want her to grow up believing she can do anything with her life. I have this unaccountable desire to be free."

"What can I do to help?"

"You have always been such a good friend."

"Where to now? Let me help you get started."

"I was hoping you would say that. Thank you." Her voice broke and he waited till she composed herself enough to continue. "I want to relocate to someplace warmer."

"New York is definitely out then." He chuckled, looking out at the city from his office window.

"Denton, Texas."

"Denton, Texas? Where the heck is that place?"

"You should know—it's just north of Dallas."

"Of all the places in the world, why there?"

"Because we stopped there on our road trip to Corpus, remember?"

"Not really."

"I remember it clearly. We stopped for gas. I was hungry so we ate at this cute little mom-and-pop restaurant. We even visited a few shops. It's a cute town. All artsy. It reflects who I am. Who I want to be."

"I guess those reasons are as good as any." He laughed.

"It also has two universities."

"Does that mean you will finish your degree?"

"Yes, that's my plan. Long time coming, Simon. I seem to keep getting sidetracked by bad marriage decisions, but no more."

"No more marriages for either one of us." He agreed.

"But you've never been married."

"There are two marriages between us. I believe that's enough."

She laughed. "Agreed. Never again."

She and Zeba moved.

Phone calls between them began again. Every day. He listened to her excitement of being single. Of finding who she was post-marriage. She told him in detail about this little place she and Zeba had moved into and how she was transforming it and making the space work for them. The Alice he knew returned. The town and her place sounded so intriguing that he had to come see it. They spent a week together, talking, eating, sightseeing, and doing fun activities with Zeba. It was as though they had formed this little platonic family unit. Although they never crossed the line of romance, Simon felt they had something better, more enduring; friendship.

At first, Alice didn't want to date, but with Simon's encouragement, she gave in. Maybe she'd find someone worthy, but secretly hoped she wouldn't. Yeah, he messed up. And then, because he wouldn't allow himself to have her again—to keep from hurting her, the idea of writing about her—again came about. It was a way to remain close. And magazines bought it up. There was also the mention of 'Blanche' as single mom bringing up Zeba (Zinnia) and Alice's lack of finding true love, plus the awkward, funny dates. And as a result, the relationship made him a famous columnist. It was then the decision to move to Texas was made in order to be a part of their lives when not on the road.

It seemed nearly impossible that over twenty years had passed since then. And now, Zeba was grown and ready for her own marriage. Alice with graying hair, and lines on her face made her even more attractive. And at the helm of her very own struggling antique business. And he, living the dream in Denton, Texas. Still best friends with Alice. Unrequited love was the best kind for them. No delusions. No tears. No heartbreak. And a secret to be kept from Zeba.

Simon returned to bed.

His cell rang. He looked at the clock. Barely 3 a.m. *Who the hell is calling me at this time?*

"Hello?"

"Simon." She sobbed.

"Fiona."

Chapter 14

Alice
A week later
7 AM

Up early, Alice had bathed, powdered, and perfumed, already packed and feeling joyful. As she waited for her self-painted nails to dry, she sat by the open window and watched the billowing curtain. The breeze felt sensuous on her skin. Alice tossed a notebook into her purse so she could write down her own personal experiences and not have Simon do all the translation. She had a voice too and it was time to be heard. At this moment in time, all was right in the world. Zeba was engaged to a kindhearted man—albeit a mediocre chef—taking on the responsibility of her shop, plus Thalia's baby room.

Most of all, Simon was home, and packing, perhaps at this very moment. Could he be thinking of her? What were his aspirations for this trip? Hopefully he was thinking of what this journey might mean for them as a couple, too. Driving down the road, just the two of them, away from everyone and everything, all her concerns blowing away in the breeze with the top down. Of course they'd get closer. Today, she was going away with her friend and imagining renewing what they once had. "Just you and me, babe." And the hours and hours of talking together that awaited.

Chapter 15

Fiona
Same Day

"Here I am, Simon! Straight from the beauty parlor. I've been pedied and manied and even got my hair fixed. How do I look?" In pink flowy slacks and an embroidered hippie-style top, thirty-something Fiona whirled about, kicking up her sandaled feet one at a time while splaying her fingers.

"You look fine. Just fine." Simon squinted his eyes against the summer sun, shifting on one leg and then the other.

"Thanks, Simon, but I think I look better than 'fine'." On her second twirl about, she noticed a woman approaching. The long-haired woman wore a twisted ponytail with gray strands cascading about her shoulders. She supposed she meant to do that but wasn't sure why since she herself preferred the more buttoned-up look. There was a slight limp in the woman's step as she dragged along two large white suitcases.

Simon welcomed this person with a kiss on the cheek.

It was then Fiona figured out who she was. "You must be Alice." She embraced her with a two-arm, full bosom hug.

Alice seemed startled by the warm greeting, which Fiona found quite puzzling. Then as if she should know who she was, she announced, "I'm Fiona."

"Nice to meet you, Fiona." Alice gave Simon a puzzled look.

"Thanks." It was then Fiona noticed Alice's nose was kind of funny looking—almost too large for her face. Her hair was a pretty shade of gray, but still gray. Alice's makeup also needed a freshening. Just because the woman was older didn't mean she shouldn't keep up on maintenance. "Oh, Alice, you're the one. Simon told me all about you and how he broke your heart. Poor thing. Simon, why'd you break her heart? Tell me that story again."

"Simon? Break my heart? I don't think so." Alice guffawed, looking suddenly angry as she hit his arm."Background information may or may not be true, especially coming from this man."

"No worries. I got your back, girl." Fiona's elbow jabbed Alice, causing her to stumble. "Us women must stick together."

"Excuse us both for a moment, Fiona. We won't be long." Simon guided Alice a few steps away.

"You two go ahead. I will wait right here for you," Fiona called out. "Take your time. It's not as hot here as it is back home. Whoa, you remember how hot it was there, Simon?"

"It's plain to see why you spent so much time away." Alice shoved Simon away as he tried to walk her down the street.

"Yeah, I do remember, give us a second, Fiona. Hey, Alice, I gave background information." Simon rubbed his arm. "I guess that was a mistake."

"You guess it was a mistake?" She gave him another shove. "Who is this woman and exactly what did you say about me?" Alice asked while shooting a fake smile in Fiona's direction.

"There's something you should know." Simon cleared his throat again.

Alice heaved a heavy sigh.

"I met her while in—"

"New Orleans," Alice finished, as her face flushed red.

"We met about a month ago," Fiona pointed out, now standing right next to them having heard the entire conversation.

"She arrived yesterday," Simon went on to say.

"You make me sound like I am delivered cargo."

"Hardly," Alice mused. "I'd use a different descriptor if it were left up to me."

"Alice, be nice."

"I think I can clear up this situation. Simon asked me to ride along, and he'd give me a lift back home at the end."

The glare off the bank of windows was searing. Alice shielded her eyes by cupping her right hand over her brow. "Must've had some good times."

"We sure did." Now she gave Simon's hand a squeeze. "I hope you're okay about me going along. Simon said it would be okay." Fiona held her hands together in a prayerful manner.

"Well, if Simon says it's all right then who am I to say anything different? You two go on without me. I'll stay right here in Denton. I've got a lot on my plate." Alice turned on her heels and again dragged the suitcases bumping along on the pavement behind.

"Fiona, please stay put right here. Alice!" Simon called as he hurried down the street after her.

"Alice." Fiona cupped her hands around her mouth. "Stop. I see you are upset about this situation, so I won't go along."

"You are going, Fiona," Simon hollered as pedestrians stopped to stare. "And you are too, Alice. Alice, did you hear me? You're both coming along."

Alice fumbled with keys trying to unlock the shop.

"You just can't back out now. Please," Simon begged, catching up to her with Fiona tagging along behind with her suitcases. "The whole purpose of the trip is you. Without you, there is no reason to go."

"*C'est la vie.* That's life." Now inside the shop, Alice stared at the back wall. "What is Stella doing?"

"Huh?" Simon looked around.

"Who is Stella?" Fiona asked turning in circles to find her.

"My assistant." Alice narrowed her eyes at Stella who was clearing a shelf of vintage kitchen gadgets to replace with new boxed cooking products. "I haven't even left town and you're already rearranging my shop?"

Stella turned about and smiled sheepishly from the step ladder. "Alice, I thought you left."

"Obviously. What's this all about?" Alice placed both hands on her hips as the suitcases on either side of her tipped over.

"Zeba and I had this wonderful idea. Didn't she tell you?" Stella gingerly got off the ladder.

"No, she did not," Alice bristled.

"That's odd, she told me you agreed. Not only did she say you agreed but loved the idea."

"What idea is that?"

Zeba breezed through the front door and looked surprised to see everyone. "Mom, I thought you were leaving first thing this morning?"

"Zeba, what's this all about?" Alice pointed.

"Yes, isn't it great? Mom, there are several stores on the square that hold classes. Down the street, The Art Studio teaches painting, stained glass, drawing, gel prints, and jewelry making during the day and evening hours. Another shop across the square gives lessons on furniture painting. Other stores are following suit as to their expertise. Since there is a nice kitchen in the back here, we thought we could hold cooking classes with Martin as chef. You know he needs a job, and it would be nice to also offer updated cooking supplies. Bring more customers in too."

"I do believe Zeba has a great idea. Get rid of all this junk and bring in the new, updated stuff. Hi, Zeba, I'm Fiona. Simon and I met in New Orleans and I'm going on a trip with him and your mom."

Zeba looked at Fiona and gave a weak smile.

The store bell rang as Martin walked in pulling a cart with boxed kitchen supplies.

"Martin. So, you Stella, and you Zeba, all feel you can turn my shop into a restaurant while I'm gone? Without my permission?"

"New person. Hi. Who are you? Let me introduce my person to you. I'm Fiona." Fiona turned to Martin.

"I'm Martin, ma'am," Martin held out his hand. "Nice to meet you."

"Soon to be Alice's son-in-law," Simon whispered.

"I'm Fiona, Simon and Alice's friend."

"Not a restaurant. Cooking classes. It will be good

for business," Stella protested. "Look, since you don't like this, then Zeba can take all this inventory back and recall all the flyers."

"There are flyers too?" Alice ran her fingers through her hair.

"Mom, I'm not about to take back all the new cooking pans and sets of kitchen aids. I have a plan."

"Plans are always good," Fiona chirped. "Let youth speak. We shall listen."

"Who did you say you are again?" Zeba asked the new woman.

"Hi, I'm Fiona."

"Zeba is my daughter," Alice answered. "Clearly, she has a plan, but not all plans are good. Some go awry. So, Zeba, you feel you can take care of this new venture in my store, along with helping Stella, and designing Talia's baby room?"

"No problem." Stella stood her ground.

"Come on, Alice. Things are in good hands. Let's go." Simon tugged at her. "We're losing time."

"I simply cannot leave town in good conscience with cooking classes going on behind my back," Alice grizzled. "There're too many elements that can go wrong and I won't be here to fix any of it when it does."

"You have committed to this trip, Alice. Don't back out now." Simon frowned.

"Mom, go!" Stella reached for the door and flung it open. "I can handle it all. Trust me, will you? And this woman could turn out to be your best friend."

"You really think so?" Fiona gushed. "I'd love that."

Martin picked up her suitcases and walked them to

the open door where he set them down.

"This has certainly been a morning of surprises."Alice looked from Fiona to Stella to Zeba to Simon back to Martin. "I usually enjoy meeting new people."

"Maybe I'm the cause of all this trouble." Fiona tip-toed closer as her stomach tied into a knot.

"You are the cause of one problem, but not the cause of this particular problem." Alice raised a brow.

"Alice, please let us try this. What can it hurt?" Stella looked as though she might burst into tears. "And if you stay because of me, I will quit. That is what I will do. I will quit."

"Let's all just simmer down," Simon insisted.

"Very well. Okay, let's try it for the summer. When I return, in a few weeks, we will re-evaluate it."

"Alice, we will be on the road for a few months," Simon said.

"Perhaps you and Fiona will be on the road for a few months, but I may be on the road for a few weeks."

"That's not what you agreed to."

"And this," Alice nodded toward Fiona who was examining her nails, "was not what I agreed to."

"Book deal. House. Money." Simon's eyes grew wide.

"Okay. I will go. But before you two ladies make any more major decisions, run it past me first. I am the owner. That goes for you too, Martin."

"Of course," Martin replied.

"Of course, Mom. Now off you go and have a lovely time." Stella scooted them all back to the street and Zeba slammed the shop door.

Simon turned to Fiona who wasn't moving.

"Fiona, come. We're getting a late start as it is."

"Thanks for the invite, Simon, but maybe I should be the one to stay back here, and you two scoot. I am all turned around, so point me in the direction of the bus depot, give me a little shove to get my feet moving, and I will be on my way back home." Fiona looked from one to the other, hoping someone would speak up to say they really, *really* wanted her to come, too.

"I'm at a loss for how to interpret this situation, nor do I know how to answer. Simon and I are supposed to be on a business trip and here you are, ready for a vacation in your flip-flops. Not what I expected. Not at all. But today seems to be a day of surprises. All on me."

"I must appear like an unforeseen tractor tipped sideways on a one-lane road during a hurricane. Or a tornado. You have tornados here. We get hurricanes where I come from. Simon told me all about you this morning at breakfast, and I said I just cannot wait to meet that girl and all her beaus." Fiona tumbled her words.

"So, you two had breakfast together?" Alice put her hands on her hips, wondering what else they ate.

Chapter 16

"It's not what you think," Simon said.

"Since you seem to know everything, what am I thinking?"

Simon remained silent.

"Fiona, why would you want to come along? What's your story?"

Feeling agitated, Fiona took a giant step back. "Why? Because it sounded like fun, that's why. And I don't think I have a story."

"Fun? Fun to listen to some stranger's past mess-ups?"

"You are putting it into book form for the public to read, right?" Fiona shot back.

"Ladies. Let's stop talking and get going. You can argue in the car."

"It's obvious you do not care for me. I'm not sure why either. Usually, people like me straight off and I become their favorite person in no time at all."

"I believe that. You and Simon sure hit it off pretty quickly."

"I'll have you know that I won Miss Congeniality in the Miss New Orleans pageant twenty years back." Fiona ignored the preceding comment.

"Fiona, don't take this personally. I do not know you enough not to like you."

"True. Let's get to know one another. We can do

that by taking this trip together. Clearly, you want to make this life journey, or you wouldn't be standing here, packed and ready to go, and acting all prissy piss."

"I am not acting prissy piss. I do not act prissy or piss. I do not ever say those words. In fact, I have never heard that phrase ever in my life. You must know me before you can judge me and my actions," Alice snipped.

"Alice, take a breath. We need Fiona. She must come. She's the photographer."

"Whoa, I am?" Confused, Fiona whirled about silently mouthing the words to herself as her left hand flew to her chest. The revelation was a new one and the joy of it took away her breath.

He nodded his head.

"Alice, I am the photographer, I have to come." Excited about her new title, Fiona suddenly took her new role very seriously. "I'm sure you are on edge because you just found out that your shop has been taken over by two or three innovative people with progressive ideas, plus you probably haven't had your morning coffee before meeting me. It's understandable."

"I never drink coffee."

"Oh. No coffee. I'll make a note of it. Let's just start the day over." She wanted this woman to like her for heaven's sake. She hated not being liked. "We are here for you. Simon and I are here for you. We need to work together on this project and get along."

"Simon, I thought you were the photographer," Alice said.

"How can I take pictures and take notes?"

"A recorder on your phone. Oh, all right. I spent days packing, so I might as well go."

"Sisterhood." Fiona held out her fist to knuckle bump, but Alice slid her hands into her pockets. Not at all the carefree happy gal Simon described. Fiona wasn't so sure all the nice things Simon told her about the woman could be true. For one thing, there seemed to be no Texas hospitality to her. Maybe she was stressed. That had to be it. Or going through menopause. Hormones played ugly tricks on one's mood. It sure had on her aunt and mother. Alice needed to take some Yoga lessons to de-stress. Later she'd suggest it to her.

"Now that's settled, we will be ready to go as soon as I load Alice's things." Simon grabbed Alice's suitcases.

"Simon, do you really think we can fit all our things, plus three adults, into your sports car?" Alice asked in a shaky voice. Tears framed her eyes.

"No more cold feet, okay? It's all taken care of. I thought of everything and rented an SUV." He nodded toward the black Tucson.

"No sports car?" Alice asked.

"We will fit in it just fine. I even have a cooler with drinks and snacks."

"I call dibs on the front." Fiona hurried down the street toward the SUV and hiked up into the front seat as Alice silently slid into the back. "Where are we headed?"

After shutting the trunk, Simon came around to the front and got in. "I'm programming the GPS right now. We're heading northeast, Fiona, toward the Midwest" Simon looked at Alice through the rearview mirror. "I am ready for the address, which is—what, Alice?"

"The Midwest is the last stop."

"Okay. Last I heard we are heading toward Wisconsin, Illinois, and Arkansas?"

"Later. Right now, program your GPS toward the northwest to Wyoming."

"Oh good! I love Wyoming! Everything about Wyoming intrigues me," Fiona whelped. "This is my first time going."

"Do you have family there?" Alice asked.

"No. I've seen pictures."

"Wyoming? That's a new one." Simon cut Fiona short. "Are you switching up plans?"

"Ah, huh. We are going to see Charlie ex-number-one."

"Charlie? Why?" Simon asked looking confused, and a bit upset. "And when did he move?"

"Why? Because I just decided at this moment, I want to see him. Add him to the napkin list."

"A napkin list?" Fiona asked.

"You are sure about this?" Simon frowned with concern. "So, we have Pick 3 plus one?"

"Pick 3 plus one," Alice affirmed, giving a slight smile.

"Wyoming."

"Wyoming."

They barely eased onto I-35 North when Fiona turned in her seat. "Brave girl!" Fiona smiled at Alice, who looked away. *What a sourpuss. Why would Alice care that she came on this trip?* She looked at Simon and then back at Alice again. That's when it occurred to her that Alice must have some feelings for the man. She settled back into the front seat and got as quiet trying to figure out the situation. Her purpose was not only to have fun on the trip but also, perhaps, to help Alice figure herself out. All that raw emotion and non-coffee drinking couldn't be good for anyone. She was very good with things like that—people back home knew that about her. Why, she even helped her niece figure out her life career of becoming a waitress. She loved to wait on her husband and her kids, so why not wait on others and make some money while at it? And just like that her niece working at Café Haven became a reality.

Fiona smiled, thinking that she was more than just a tag-along. She was now the photographer and the person to help Alice find her joy. Those were important jobs. She raked through her purse; glad she had remembered to bring along the instamatic camera. It's always good to have a backup in case her eight year old cell phone goes down.

Chapter 17

Alice

It all seemed a bit too convenient—out of nowhere a woman by the name of Fiona became a key player for the trip that was meant, supposedly, just for her and Simon. This was to be their love connection trip—finally. Scratch those plans. From where she sat, looking at the back of Fiona's head to the back of Simon's head, it seemed a little suspicious. If only she had something hard to fling at them. All she had in her purse was money, credit cards, makeup, and her wallet—nothing worth losing.

At times she hated her own thoughts, like right now. Once they wormed their way into her feelings, they seemed to take root and eat away at her as they played over and over. If she could only sneak a call to Talia to vent. Getting it out of her system might make her feel better. She stared at her cell. The call was out since they sat only inches away. There was always text. Alice began texting about her dilemma.

Talia finally responded saying, whether she liked it or not, she was stuck and to try to make the best of it. A lot of good that did. Not.

"Who are you texting with back there?" Simon wanted to know.

"No one." Alice took the notebook from her purse

and began writing.

Feeling alone, with various scenarios drumming inside of her head, she had to figure out if Simon was sweet on the woman—or not. And if not, what purpose did this woman play? This was worse than trying to figure out if she had enough money to buy a new fold-out couch bed for her loft apartment. Certainly, by the end of the day, her overthinking and figuring would have worn her out. Until then, she simmered, and having Fiona around made her feel inferior. It was time to wake up to the fact that Simon would never be hers—not with thirty-something Lolita with long ginger-colored hair, wearing tiger-striped sunglasses, big boobs bursting out of her top, her bright neon pink suitcases thumping around in the way back, and sitting in the front seat laughing, saying stupid things like, "You are so clever, Simon."

Alice decided to enjoy the trip—there was simply no other choice. Probably Fiona was a very nice person and not the man-eater she imagined. Fiona was just the one who sashayed up the street and changed her plans. And yeah, she could see Fiona in a bustier playing some musical instrument—badly.

Alice wrote out her observation of Fiona in her notebook. Getting it all out on paper was a bit cathartic. After simmering down, she decided to take Talia's advice and forge ahead. Besides, no one liked negativity. She'd just put her best foot forward. Positivity was her word of the day. Alice settled back into the seat and closed her eyes, thinking about the people she'd see again, and new people she might meet. Yes, fun was on the horizon if she took the right attitude. Simon certainly didn't want to present a pouting person to the world. "Do you know what the monumental question is that one asks oneself during a relationship?"

"She speaks. Tell me." Simon laughed.

"When will I end things? Or will it be he who ends things? If I end things first, will it hurt him? If he ends things first, will I be devastated? And then decide that I really liked him after all."

"How old are you?" Fiona asked.

Alice opened her eyes and sat forward, hiding her notebook from Fiona's hawk eyes. "It doesn't matter the age because we are always worried about being hurt and hurting another in any relationship. Even married couples go through this. I know this."

"But lots of married folk work hard to keep their marriage," Fiona said.

"Everything sours after a while. Cream, milk—people. Simon, perhaps you could sometime do a study on married people and what keeps them together."

"One book at a time."

"You know; I've been reading Simon's blog for years; "Dating Blanche." So clever."

"And you happened to stumble upon this genius blogger in person."

"Yes, Exactly right," Fiona said. "And here we are. Or rather, here I am, with the famous blogger but where is this Blanche, the subject of his entries."

"That's me." Alice waved at her.

"Impossible. Blanche is my kinda gal. Fun-loving, sense of humor, certainly not dark and sullen. Oh well. I guess that's called a writer's privilege to shape people into what he wants them to be, or at least to get them to read his column. But this is a moment of disappointment for me to find out that Blanche isn't Blanche. She's Alice."

Alice closed her eyes pretending to sleep.

"So, you are Blanche. Do you know which of your dates is my favorite?" Fiona twisted about to look at Alice. "The little person."

"Ah." A compliment. She'd take it. Alice nodded her head, eyes still shut, and smiled.

"It was so odd that he bought a drink for himself and not one for you since he invited you out," Fiona continued with her analysis.

"I thought so too. But then I got to thinking about it. He ordered the drink at the bar that he could just peek over. Maybe he said, 'Beers.' But the bartender just heard 'beer'."

"You're saying, his voice might have been muffled because his mouth didn't clear the bar."

"Or, perhaps the bartender was hard of hearing and forgot his hearing aid before he left home." Simon nodded.

"Endless possibilities," Alice agreed.

"Wasn't he part of a band playing that night?"

"Correct. He asked me to the bar to listen to his music."

"And the steps were too tall for him, so you had to help him down once the set was over."

"I did. Good thing he didn't weigh much. I have a bad hip." Alice smiled again. "And then he sat next to me. But the chair was at the next table, not at mine." Alice gasped with a new theory. "Do you suppose he was ashamed of me and didn't want to be seen with me? I feel so embarrassed."

Simon laughed. "Alice, you're projecting too

much."

"Maybe you just weren't his type."

"You're missing beautiful scenery, Fiona. Look out the window and enjoy," Simon interrupted.

Alice noticed there was a decline in traffic the further north they drove. The houses and farms were spread apart. Lots of fields, fences, trees, and sky.

"Anyone need a break? I'm about ready to stretch my legs and gas up again." Simon swung into an interstate full-service rest area.

"Whatever you want. You are the driver." Fiona smiled. "I could use a turn in the little girl's room. My doctor once told me that I have an infantile bladder so I need to use the bathroom more than normal people. "

"Let's call it a day, ladies."

Chapter 18

Alice

The next afternoon, the sun was high above the Taos Mountains. Every part of the inside of the SUV was touched by its sparkle. Alice woke up from her nap in the backseat and sleepily forced herself into an upright position. Fiona draped her hand over the back of her seat.

Alice wrinkled her brow studying her perfectly manicured turquoise nails. There were rabbit decals on the thumbs. Who had the patience for those? Then she examined her own nails. They were clean but noticed they were sloppily done. Sighing, Alice gazed out the window at the passing scenery, thinking about the purpose of this entire trip. To do justice for Simon's book, she was going to have to leave her secret safe place and open with honesty—the reason she wanted to see Charlie. She left him without much of an explanation. Back then she was too scared. Today she felt braver and decided she owed him a reason.

"Is your stomach pitching back there?" Simon asked with his eyes on the road.

"No, not car sick."

"It might be nice to stop soon for a bathroom break." Fiona pushed hair from her eyes.

"It's just about dinnertime. We'll stop soon.

Thought you might be feeling nervous."

"Yes, nerves. I hope I don't feel this way the entire trip."

Fiona offered a sympathetic smile.

"After dinner, we can get a place for the night." Simon pulled into a restaurant parking lot. "We've been driving most of the day. According to the GPS and People Finder app, Charlie is within a hundred miles. Want me to call him tonight and give a heads up, or should we just pop in?"

"Let's surprise him."

"I think it's better to call," Simon said. "I'll take care of that so you don't have to Alice."

"Wonderful."

They got out of the car and walked into the small, touristy restaurant, packed with dead animal mounts on knotty pine walls.

Waiting for their food to arrive, Alice looked at Fiona to make small talk and break the frozen three-inch ice between them. "Have you always lived in Louisiana?"

"Yes, ma'am."

"What do you do for a living?" Alice sipped her water.

"I'm a meter maid."

"Are you a musician too? What instrument do you play?" Alice asked.

"No hobbies of any kind. I do sing in the church choir."

Alice lifted her eyebrows. "How did you get interested in photography?"

Simon shifted in his seat and gave her a sideways look, which Fiona didn't seem to notice.

"I've always liked taking pictures. It's fun."

"Pictures, is like a hobby then, I suppose." Alice moved her silverware around on the tabletop. "I noticed you haven't taken any pictures of this trip yet. Highly unusual whose passion is photography. Not of the countryside, or of us traveling together—or me. I'd think you'd want hundreds of pictures for Simon to select from."

"You know; you are exactly right." Fiona began digging through her large bag. "I think I will get my camera out and start snapping away right now. Thanks, Alice."

"Good thing you've been taking pictures along the way, Simon," Alice told him under her breath.

Fiona pulled the camera from her purse. Immediately, she held the instamatic up to her eye and snapped a picture of Alice, who burst into laughter. "You're kidding, right? I was talking about your professional camera. You have a great sense of humor. I need to appreciate you more."

"What? But this is my camera. My only one—oh wait, I do have a camera on my cell phone if someone can explain to me how to access it." Fiona seemed perplexed.

"Simon just said you're a professional photographer but that is your camera?"

"This is my camera."

"Simon. An instamatic? Really?" Alice seethed. "What's her purpose on this trip if not for photography?"

Fiona looked toward Simon as though waiting for an answer.

"Alice, Fiona wanted to come along. So, I gave her

112

a job."

"A very important job." Alice was stressed. "Please excuse me. I need a moment alone."

"Want me to take that moment alone with you, Alice?"

"You're the reason for my stress. So, no."

"Alice." Simon narrowed his gaze.

Alice ignored them and headed to the bathroom.

"Fiona, wait here." Simon followed Alice.

"Go away, Simon." Alice tried shutting the door in his face, but he jammed his foot in the doorway.

"Please don't be mad."

"Mad? What were you thinking, Simon? The photographs will tell a story as much as your words. Are we even doing this book?"

"Yes, we are."

"Where is your camera now?"

"It's in the back of the car."

"Get it. I think the book needs a few heads in it." Alice sarcastically whined and pushed open the door to the commode.

When she returned to the table, she didn't like what she saw. The back of Simon and Fiona huddled together. He had his arm around her shoulder.

"Maybe now I know the role Fiona plays on this trip," Alice mused, sliding back into the booth.

Fiona wiped tears from her face.

"What's wrong with Ansel Adams?" Alice asked Simon.

"I know what you are thinking, and you have it all wrong, Alice." Simon's voice was harsh.

"Well, if I do, it's because someone has been less than honest with me."

"Okay, here it goes." Simon took a breath and removed his arm from around Fiona. He folded his hands on the table. "When I went to New Orleans last month, I wanted to experience a side of the city I didn't know—kind of looking for lost souls."

"That explains Fiona."

"Alice, be kind. This isn't like you."

"I'll behave. Go on."

"I was driving down this narrow street and saw an interesting stone chapel. I was caught in traffic, I couldn't move, and then I realized it was a funeral procession. I did my best to find a place to park and then I walked back. I met Fiona. It was her husband's funeral."

"Oh, I didn't know. I am so very sorry, Fiona." Shame engulfed Alice in an instant. Simon was trying to be a friend, and she had been a full-blown green-eyed bitch. Her voice softened. "When?"

"About five weeks." Fiona dabbed at her eyes as the waitress set their food in front of them, then left.

"I crashed the funeral, so to speak. I took pictures with my 'professional' camera, which I left in the car this evening." Simon rolled his eyes at Alice.

"Again, I am very sorry for your loss, Fiona, and for treating you badly."

"Does that mean we can be friends?" Fiona perked up.

"Let's take that one day at a time."

"Thanks. My Bubby and I only dated a few weeks before we decided to get married."

"Love at first sight, how romantic." Alice tried to smile. "How long were you married, if you don't mind me asking?"

Fiona wept. "We were married a few weeks. He was a police officer."

"Oh, no, did he die in the line of duty?" Alice faced Fiona.

"No. It was after the line of duty. He came home and dropped dead on our brand-new shag carpeting, of a heart attack."

"The funeral was impressive with all the Blue. And I saw Fiona, leaning against the old stone church, crying."

"Is this where I get all weepy?" Alice whispered under her breath.

"He was just standing there, staring at me, so I asked him what he was doing, and we started this conversation."

"I'm so glad Simon comforted you." Alice looked from Simon, who obviously was angry with her, to the weeping widow. And then there was Alice in the middle, the slutty faux woman with a past.

"Thanks. That means so much to me, Alice. As it turned out, I became his tour guide and drove him around New Orleans. It helped me get my mind off things."

"I bet Simon did." Alice drummed her fingers on the table.

"I had packed up to leave, but when I met Fiona, I stayed for another month."

"Oh. two months? Interesting."

"When Simon left for Texas, I suddenly felt this black cloud drop over me again. I couldn't shake it. A week later, I took a bus to Denton on a whim. I'd still like to be the professional photographer, if okay."

"How about, you can be my assistant?" Simon

suggested.

"I'd like that. It'd be just like my brother who is a plumber's assistant."

Alice didn't know how to feel. Evidently, Fiona was the type to fall in love very quickly. Was she now eyeing Simon as husband number two? And Simon always had a soft heart for women in distress. Even though Fiona was a beautiful woman, clearly, she wasn't Simon's type, but just what type he liked she wasn't sure. Even though they had been best of friends for decades, there were still unopened doors inside of Simon. Although he dated from time to time, he had always been careful to skirt those subjects—and until Fiona, she never saw him with another woman. Could Fiona turn out to be his type?

But now, she noticed the kindest in Simon, giving her a sense of purpose with the bogus title and job. Today, Alice learned something new about him. There was great compassion in helping others get over a hard bump in the road and wanted them to realize their worth. Alice learned something about herself too—she was a sarcastic bitch. Suddenly, she felt as though her frozen heart just might be melting. Time would tell. She heaved a sigh, respecting this man even more. If she ever loved again, it would be Simon. But she couldn't love again, because she still loved Simon.

They found a small hotel for the night. The place had a Western-Native American motif minus dead head mounts. Their rooms were next to one another with adjoining doors.

Fiona took her time in the bathroom, while Alice waited. She turned on the TV and watched an old newsreel from the 1950s capturing beautiful Grace

Kelly. Alice was mesmerized watching her emerge from a limo. She carried out the simplest tasks with style and poise. Legs together, skirt pulled over her knees. It was like a poem. Alice backed it up to watch how she positioned herself in the car first before her exit from the vehicle. If Alice had gone to etiquette school instead of college, as her mother suggested, she would know how to do this by now. No matter how old one got, they never knew how to do everything.

The sound of Simon moving around in his room came from behind the closed door. She felt the flash of guilt because she was withholding information concerning this trip. For now, she'd keep that information to herself. She turned to her side and shut her eyes, waiting for her turn in the bathroom. The bed was unusually comfortable. The bed covers warm and soft. The pillow didn't need to be tugged at. Her attention drifted.

There was something on her mind but couldn't quite remember what. All at once, the bed didn't feel quite right. Opening her eyes, she couldn't focus. The room was strange. She blinked a few times. The only thing she recognized was one of her suitcases was open. Confused, she sat up to get a better look as daylight poked in between the curtains. Someone in the other bed let out a loud snort.

Now she remembered. She was on a road trip with Frick and Frack, going to see one of the biggest mistakes of her life. It was a scary proposition. What was she thinking? There was also a good cause for the pain in the pit of her stomach. Seeing Charlie again made her want to lurch. With a pounding headache, she popped three aspirins while contemplating her faulty decision-making skills. The clock pointed to midnight.

Then a few flashes of light blinded her. Fiona was awake. "What in the world are you doing?"

"Taking pictures, just as you and Simon told me to do."

"With your instamatic?" Alice couldn't help but smile.

"It's the only one I have, but it's a step up from those throwaway cameras."

"And taking an aspirin is noteworthy?" She giggled.

"It's real life, Alice."

"Okay, then, take some of me now!" Alice strutted across the room, pulling her nightgown up over her knees, before flopping onto the bed and sitting up on her elbows to wink, trying to look alluring.

Fiona laughed along hysterically, taking one shot after the next. "I'm the paparazzi!"

Alice jumped on the bed and tossed a pillow in the air. "This is me destroying the room!"

"And I am recording it to post online with my cellphone as soon as you show me how!"

Alice dropped onto the bed, thrilled the tension between them had not only eased but was finally over. "Fiona, you can be a fun girl."

"I told you."

That night, Fiona slept peacefully in the next bed.

The following morning, Alice showered, dressed, and then went down to the continental breakfast of powdered eggs and cellophane-looking sweet rolls. Simon was already there downing a cup of coffee. "Did you sleep well?"

"You don't happen to have an alcoholic beverage

on you, do you?" she asked.

He gave her a wry smile. From his inside jacket pocket, he withdrew a silver flask. She grabbed it, unscrewed the top, and took a swig, choking a bit as it went down. "I slept like a baby last night," Alice said a little too brightly, wiping her mouth with the side of her hand.

"Me too. Good sleeping weather." He winked.

"Then we both slept fine. Good."

"Where's Fiona?"

"Still in bed. I didn't wake her."

"Have you checked in with the shop yet back home?"

"Of course. Spoke with Stella and Zeba. They seem excited and pressing forward. I'll call again tomorrow." Alice took another swig from the flask and then handed it back before rooting around in her purse for her cell to check messages. "Since this trip with you, it's no longer my number one fantasy to find out I've made the right choices all along."

"Really? Now that surprises me. What is your number one fantasy now?" Simon asked as though he were vaguely amused.

"Just making it back to Texas in one piece with my heart intact and to thank god each day that no one's life is tangled up in mine."

"Why would you be thankful for that?"

Alice sat quietly for a minute. "Because I am discovering my life is peaceful the way it is, that's all."

"Ah, you have Charlie nerves." He half chuckled.

"I do. Don't laugh."

"Then you are still committed to this trip?"

"Totally. May I remind you that I'm buying a

home with your book money? I need it for my old age."

"Ah, nice. I will quote you. But you will never grow old, Alice." Simon smiled a wobbly smile as he pulled out his iPad and began tap, tap, a tapping.

"If you keep spending so much time on that, I may need to have technology permanently removed from your fingertips."

She noticed he smiled at her as if seeing her for the first time in a very long time.

She liked it.

Chapter 19

Alice
37 years ago…
Wedding #1

Alice begins writing her story in the notebook:

The day after graduation, Simon took off for grander and bigger things, all of which did not include men or Eau Claire, Wisconsin. His life going forward was in New York City. And my life would be—what?

I was devastated and here came Charlie into my life, not long after Simon made his escape. Feeling vulnerable, I was ripe to find someone; nearly anyone would do in my state of mind. After all, I had to have done something wrong. Perhaps my sexual prowess was off—bad mojo. Mother had a different explanation. "You gave your milk so there was no need to buy the cow." How did the woman even know that? If that's the truth, Simon sure got buckets full. I think Mother could tell my deflowering event by just looking in my eyes. She said so time and again, and Mother was usually right.

Charlie sat across the table from me in the campus commissary giving a lengthy introduction. It was impressive. Plus, he was handsome. Plus, he drove a Grand Prix. Plus, his entire attention focused on me. His resume included being a college dropout, and now sold life insurance to college kids who felt invincible. In other words, not much money was coming in. Still, money wasn't everything, and I was surprised when he began calling.

Maybe it was time to start thinking about settling down. Since my hormones were on full blast, marriage could be the answer to my Catholic guilt of premarital sex.

It was fast. All of it. Just a few months after meeting, he told Mother he wanted to marry me. I know this because I happened to be in the room at the time.

"Are you sure about this Alice? This is what you really want?"

I just smiled and nodded as though I knew about it all along. In the next breath, we were deciding between a sit-down chicken dinner, or a smorgasbord at the reception. It was kind of exciting. The wedding planning was so much fun that I totally forgot about the marriage part.

Looking back, I knew the relationship was completely wrong, and shallow. But here I was twenty-one. And, as Mother said, someone else got the milk first—that made me spoiled milk. Nightly she lit candles so another bull would buy me and here he was. As for the sex, it wasn't very good, but it was time to stop having it out of marriage. That fault was mine. The rest of it, the abuse, was entirely his.

Even though Simon was sent a wedding invitation, plus one, not only did he not come, but he also never responded. It irked me. Where were his manners? Maybe it was just as well. There was no telling what my reaction would be if I saw him sitting in a pew, as I walked down the aisle toward Charlie. I'm sure I'd veer from the red carpet of roses and go for him. Simon still had some weird spell over me and does to this day.

The wedding happened quickly. There was nothing to be gained by waiting around. One step in my white satin shoes, after the other, holding onto Dad's arm with my streams of satin ribbon holding together the bouquet, I walked the carpet toward the altar—or the cow was led to slaughter.

The dress I wore was the first one I picked off the rack. No matter how many I tried after that, didn't compare. After all, you only fall in love once—and marry once, although soon I discovered the two didn't always go together.

And there I stood at the altar, scanning the audience for Simon, with my mind on all the Tupperware shower gifts back at the apartment, washed and neatly stacked in the kitchen cabinets. It was then I felt the preacher give a nudge.

"Huh?" My face turned hot. What did I miss?

The preacher cleared his throat. "Do you, Alice, take this man Charlie Cycle for your lawfully wedded husband, to have and to hold, in …"

I skimmed the seated guests again. Simon wasn't there. "Yes. I do."

"She cut me off," the preacher said. "She's an anxious little bride, I guess."

Laughter.

After the ceremony, I went to my childhood bedroom to change out of the gown and into a low-cut, blue party dress for the reception. At the sound of the doorknob turning, I whirled about to see Charlie standing there in the doorway with a devilish grin on his face: a wild look in his eyes.

"Hey, you." I smiled. Charlie, a few inches taller, with blonde wild curls, smiled back. He put his finger to his mouth. An uneasy embarrassment crept over me in this small room still covered in cheerleader trophies and baby dolls. It was as though I was trapped in a cage with nowhere to run. It felt so wrong being together like this in my parents' house. Yet, this was my husband. It would be okay. We were legally married. "Just starting to unzip myself, but it's stuck."

"Let me help." The young groom strode across the room, smile gone, eyes locked on his destination. No expression. Chilling. Afraid, I stepped back. His hands were rough as he moved me to the bed and pushed me down. Immediately, he climbed on board.

After a half dozen thrusts, he quickly finished with a groan and dropped like a dead man on top, where he remained for several minutes catching his breath. Beads of his sweat soaked my skin. It all had happened so fast.

"I'll just get my clothes now and change in the bathroom across the hall. Love you."

"Love you too," I murmured.

Abruptly, he stood, picked up his pants and walked out—half naked, buttocks jiggling, then closed the door behind quietly. I remained on the bed—still feeling the weight of his body. Transfixed on the ceiling light, my legs remained spread apart. What just happened? I needed to be somewhere else. I heard sounds of waves. I smelled salt water. And then there was Simon. He kissed me so gently. And then his image faded. Where are you, Simon? Take me with you.

The honeymoon was strained. They rented a cottage in Door County, Wisconsin on Clark Lake.

Totally alone with him, it was then I realized we had nothing to say to one another. During the ten-day rental, we drove in silence around the peninsula. I lost everything marrying him. But, didn't know the extent until months later.

"Can we stop to eat?" I said cheerfully. It was the beginning to act the opposite of how I felt. I became a pretender. "The eggs I made for us this morning are long since gone. Aren't you hungry by now too?"

"We can stop at a grocer and get something for you to make."

"But it's our honeymoon. I'd rather not cook."

He stared straight ahead. Gently, he said, "My mom cooks for my dad every day. You will too. Eating out is a waste of money."

Alice stopped writing and slid the notebook back into her purse. She closed her eyes, remembering how all her other suggestions of hiking trails, visiting shops, seeing a movie, and taking a boat ride on Lake Michigan were all ignored. However, there were plenty of bait stores, so they went to one. Neither of them fished so they walked around and around the store looking at nothing in particular. The place stunk of worms and fish. The big purchase was a green cooler, which still remained empty. Why her parents don't get rid of it, she will never know.

They even still had the postcards she mailed home of all the Door County places she wanted to visit—acting as though they had been there. Pretending her honeymoon was everything she ever wanted. Pretending her life was idyllic. Pretending she was the consummate wife, and Charlie her prince.

Sex. How she hated it. Perhaps it was her

punishment for the bedtime fun she had with Simon during the best spring break of her entire life. But that was done and over, and she was a married woman now with a list of wifely duties presented by her new husband, dictated by his mother.

With little income, they moved into the attic space above his parent's living room. She spent most evenings watching late-night shows and munching popcorn on the couch beside his parents, while Charlie went out with his friends. He also drank too much. The touch of his hands on her late at night when he got home still made her nauseous whenever she thought about it, even now. She turned her head to get away from his alcohol breath. His kisses were gross. The rest of her life looked like a pitch-black endless abyss.

There are all kinds of loss. You lose your teeth, you lose your dog, friendships, and even one's life. Some get lost. And that was Alice. She was lost. Lost in life.

Just when hope was nearly gone, she saw her escape. Thankfully, Charlie decided to visit his cousin a hundred miles away without her. She acted normal watching him pack. Even threw in a pout or two for good measure because he wouldn't take her along. She sat with his parents watching the clock until they went to bed at 11 p.m. It was then she took the steps two at a time to the attic, where she pulled her suitcase from the closet, and packed a few clothes. It was important to travel light. She looked around the room at everything she had to leave behind. Her laptop. Books. Extra clothes. It all could be easily replaced. Slowly, she opened the window and gently released the handle of the suitcase dropping it silently into the bushes below.

Goodbye unhappy life. Goodbye Tupperware.

The two-mile walk to the bus station helped clear her head. With each step, she took deep breaths. Once there, she called Simon for help. Naturally, she didn't expect him to drive to get her all the way from New York to Wisconsin. He did call the bus station and bought a ticket for her. Money would be waiting once she got to Chicago by way of wire at the station. Just needed to show her ID.

There was so much energy and life percolating inside that she felt she could fly. Waiting for the bus, she cried; cried due to heartbreak, cried because she missed Simon, and cried with relief to be away from Charlie and his family. Dreams of owning a business and decorating came back into view.

At her parents' house, her mother spent days trying to convince her it was just the first-year marriage jitters. She needed to go back to her husband. To make matters worse, Charlie showed up at the end of his cousin's visit, repentant, teary-eyed, swearing he'd be a good husband, begging her to return to him. She refused. Alice moved out of her parent's home into a little hovel of an apartment, again with Simon's help. But Charlie found her. She moved again, and he found her again. And then, one day, he seemed to stop searching. Obviously, he found someone new.

Alice found work as a receptionist at a resort in Milwaukee, Wisconsin. Although the salary was minimum wage, she didn't mind. Freedom was priceless, and Alice didn't mind the minimum wage salary. After paying rent for a boardinghouse room, plus a small penitence more for utilities, the meager rest belonged to her. Alice loved the twelve-by-ten room with blue painted walls, a tallboy dresser, and a narrow iron bed tucked under the eaves of the house. The bathroom was down the hall with five adults sharing. Alice carried a cleanser with her nearly each time she visited the bathroom. She was happy. On an adventure. Getting stronger.

It was hard going when all she could afford to eat were basically Romaine noodles and Spam. Her clothes were secondhand picks.

Never did she ever see Charlie again. Until today. Today she was the one who came knocking at the door.

Chapter 20

Alice
Charlie's House

It's not always prudent to assume that just because the outward appearance of your life appears unscathed, the past is where you left it.

Down a narrow gravel path, wide enough for only one car, and a slight curve, there was a small cabin. They stopped yards in front of the dwelling, beneath a canopy of pine trees.

Terrified, Alice bravely led the way to be the first to knock on the door. Maybe today his pistol wasn't loaded. Maybe he wasn't watching out the window for them.

The door creaked open. A look of surprise settled across his face in a heavy cloud. "Alice? That can't be you. You look—old."

"Hi, Charlie. Didn't you know I was coming?"

"Oops. I forgot to call," Simon whispered from behind.

"I'd know you anytime and you've gained some weight. Your hair is gray. Got old on me too." The familiar stranger stepped aside to allow them entrance.

It was crazy to walk into the lion's den especially since it took all her courage to fight her way out. The passage of years didn't matter. Suddenly she was that frightened young woman all over again because Charlie remained the evil presence that still took up residence in her mind.

A woman stared at them and then finally spoke. "Hi, Charlie's wife here, I'm Megan. Anyone hungry? How about a snack?" Her voice was thick and had mileage on it. Megan's dark hair was threaded with a bit of gray, that free-flowed down her back then clipped into a high ponytail accentuating her tall, thin build. Her face was plain and void of makeup.

"Nice to meet you. Please don't go to any trouble," Fiona bubbled, clasping her hands together.

"No trouble at all." Megan shot a broad smile.

"Then that would be fine. Can I be of any help?" Fiona overflowed with good nature.

Alice figured it was most likely due to her pink camouflage outfit that cheered her just being in it. It's all she talked about ever since breakfast.

"I'm nearly finished. Thanks for the offer anyway."

"I'm Alice." She held out her hand.

"Nice to meet you wife number one."

In Megan's brown eyes, Alice noticed shyness that she had expected, and happiness, which she had not. Megan crossed the room to shake everyone's hands before returning to her spot in the open kitchen.

"Alice, why have you returned?" Charlie muttered, scratching his chin. "We settled business long ago."

Alice searched his gaze before nodding, all the while wishing she could think of something clever to say to lighten the situation and elevate her mood. She remained silent.

"We were going to be in the neighborhood," Fiona spoke up.

"Where in the world did you come from? That accent is awful," Charlie grumbled.

"Charlie, stop being rude to our guests," Megan bossed. "Pardon my husband, I am glad you all are here."

Alice took a seat next to her spur-of-the-moment support group, scrunching in between Fiona and Simon, who all sat in a straight line on Charlie Cycle's plaid sofa. Alice couldn't take her eyes off the rifle hanging on the wall. Of course, it would take him a minute or two to stand, walk to it and remove it from over the fireplace. She'd bet money it was loaded. Next, Alice spied what looked like a gun stuffed down the side of his seat cushion, within easy reach. This was a quiet country spot, surrounded by trees and sky. No neighbors within eye or earshot.

Simon leaned back into the couch, hands folded in his lap, giving an air of ease. With his salt and pepper hair and recently pressed jeans, he looked fetching and distinguished, despite his noticeable fascination of being here. Simon held Charlie's stare, which quickly morphed into something like a glare.

Alice fidgeted with her hair. It was then she noticed perspiration marks from her underarms ruining her cotton blend blouse. She rubbed her sweaty hands along the sides of her jeans. If only someone said something more maybe she could calm down. Anxiety made her breathing flutter in the uncomfortable silence. Too overraught this morning with nerves, she passed on breakfast, and now her stomach loudly grumbled.

"I hear someone's tummy. Just hold on a minute more," Megan sang out while dumping coffee into a filter and pouring water into a machine.

"Cute place." Alice noticed the log cabin was chilly, tidy, and aroma-free. If she had to describe the home to someone, she'd say it was nicely decorated in all the usual furnishings one would expect when living in the north woods; antler lamps, bear-printed curtains, bear knickknacks, and cutesy cut-outs of fir trees. Looking carefully around at the décor and the cabin structure, she tried to imagine living here—if she were still his wife.

"We like it," Charlie said.

"We do," Megan agreed from the open kitchen where she worked, humming as she arranged a charcuterie platter. Several times she looked over at them and timidly smiled. If Alice hadn't served time as Charlie's wife, she'd regard them as the idyllic couple; Charlie the head of the household running things and Megan happy with that arrangement, needing someone to constantly serve. However, she doubted someone could really change his anger that dramatically without some sort of exorcism.

Being on wooded property like this, Alice's imagination ran wild with daunting possibilities. If Charlie chose to murder them, there'd be plenty of places to dispose of bodies in the woods. After all, no one knew they had a change of plans and headed here. Looking around at faces, she tried to read body language. Simon was too calm, but his eyes remained on Charlie. Now Megan hummed too loudly in a most annoying manner. Fiona matched that mood, but instead of humming, she shook her right leg and kept talking about how cute the cabin was until Alice wanted to duct tape her mouth shut. Charlie looked just plain pissed. It was too late to renege about changing her mind about closure. She didn't want it or need it anymore. She was just fine as is and wanted to get back on the road. Who would they see next?

"You lucked out, you know. This is Charlie's day off," Megan said, carrying rattling cups and saucers on a tray and then distributing them. "Usually, he works from dawn till dusk."

"Thank you for seeing us." Simon squeezed Alice's hand, as though saying, *I'm here. I'll keep you safe.*

And then there was Charlie, across the room in his large king-like recliner, who looked down on them all, with a hefty German shepherd at his feet Alice just noticed. "Yep, I've been a park ranger at Yellowstone for about ten years now," he said."I hand out brochures to the tourists. Moved out here years ago when my dad died. Bought this cabin with the inheritance."

"Sorry to hear. How'd he pass?" Alice asked.

"Sounds interesting. Your job that is." Fiona quickly clarified. "I bet you meet all kinds of interesting people."

"That I do, that I do." He sat cross-legged and hit his boot. "Want to hear some stories?"

"No, that's okay. We're good. Don't want to bring your work home," Simon jumped in.

Alice snickered. It was the first time Simon turned down hearing a story.

"How's your mom?" Alice asked.

"In a nursing home. Not far from here. Can you believe she called elder care on me? On Me?" Charlie responded. "What brought you here, again today, Alice? The last I knew, there was a restraining order out on me."

"That's right. I'm sure it's not in effect anymore." Alice did her best not to feel defensive while wondering if there had been an expiration date, or even if they could expire on their own. A minor technicality she had totally forgotten about.

"Is this a social call, or what?" He scratched along his thinning hairline.

Not wanting him to know the gut truth, Alice came up with a slightly different version she hoped would be more palatable to her ex. "Well—I just want to settle my past. Charlie, I wish I'd been braver when I left and directly. Okay, now that I've had my say, we can be on our way. How about it everyone?"

"If you wanted to leave so bad, I would have dropped you on your keester at the bus station myself."

"I remember fearing you. And now I no longer do. I wish you and Megan well. Anyone need to use the restroom before hitting the road again?"

"Alice, you sound like one of those positive thinking infomercials on Sunday morning TV," Fiona said.

"Speaking of Alice, I'm writing a book about her. I would like to include you Charlie in one of the chapters, that is, if it's okay with you. I have a release for you to sign here." Simon handed him the form. "If you will."

"What's this release about again?"Charlie complained looking over the contract. "And I don't get any money for it? Is that what you are saying?"

"We aren't paying anyone, but Alice. Her life, her story," Simon explained.

Megan set the charcuterie board in the middle of the coffee table and then eased down into a rocker when

Alice noticed she looked pencil-thin. A safety pin held her skirt together.

Alice looked longingly at the front door knowing what was about to happen couldn't be good. While waiting, she slipped a bit of food onto a napkin.

"Only Alice gets paid? Doesn't sound quite fair to me, Alice getting her glory told, and all the money too." After shoving a few crackers into his mouth, Charlie licked his fingers. "I think I need some compensation for breaking my heart when she left me."

"Didn't you just say you were happy when she left, Charlie?" Megan asked.

Fiona scooted to the edge of the couch to reach for a piece of cheese. "It's about choosing paths and experiences. For instance, that happened when you and Alice married and then divorced. Tell us. How did that affect you?"

"It embarrassed the hell out of me, that's what." He snapped a baby carrot in two. "It would have been better if I never married her. Put that in her book."

Alice's back muscles tensed. Her foot twitched nervously. It was hard to swallow.

The shepherd gave a low growl for which he got a touch on the head from Charlie, then immediately stopped.

"I see you still demand that women and dogs obey you," Alice snapped.

"Okay, let's all calm down here." Simon stood and got between them.

"Moving along, let me rephrase. What you learned from your failed marriage to Alice, does it affect the way you treat your second wife?"

Megan stared at the floor.

"Is this a self-help book you're writing, or what?" Charlie asked.

"I have a few questions." Fiona bravely cleared her throat.

"Fiona?" Alice glared at the woman.

"It's okay, Alice. I'm good at getting information out of people. I've been in therapy for ten years. Let me try this one more time," Fiona said. "Did it empower you to be a better husband the second time around?"

"Well said," Alice whispered to Fiona, hoping to quiet her down. Pressing Charlie for some answer he didn't want to give only made him madder.

"Third," he corrected. "Megan, she's my third."

"Third," the three on the couch simultaneously repeated.

"What happened to number two?" Alice asked with growing dread as she imagined a corpse swinging from a tree somewhere close. There were only three of them in the room who had first-hand experience with Charlie's temperament; Charlie, Megan, and herself. The others were only spectators. Since Charlie hadn't responded, Alice asked again, "Wife number two? Where is she now?"

"Anyone for lemonade? Tea? I have both," Megan offered, standing to her feet while smoothing out her skirt.

"Died," Charlie answered.

"How interesting. A divorce and then came a death," Fiona summarized. "What happened?"

"I have my camera in the car. I'd like to get it to take some shots, if you don't mind," Simon cut in.

"No need. I have my instamatic right here, somewhere, if I can only find it." Fiona dug through her purse.

"Ah, let's go for the professional camera this time," Simon said.

"Why, I think that would be very nice, right, Charlie?" said his present wife. "It could make us famous—I mean, *you* famous, so go ahead and sign that piece of paper, Charlie."

"I'll get that camera, Simon! Since I'm the assistant, it's my job." Fiona placed her fifth cracker smeared with cream cheese and olives at the edge of the paper plate and started to the door.

"Maybe I should help you with that." Alice started to get up, but Simon put his hand on her leg to stay.

While Alice watched Fiona leave, it occurred to her that perhaps Fiona also thought being murdered was a definite possibility. Alice filled with escape envy.

"May I offer dessert? There's a freshly baked cherry pie. It's Charlie's favorite. His mother's recipe."

"His mother's recipe? Did you say 'his mother's recipe?" Alice rose from her seat.

"Ah-huh." Megan nodded.

Alice laughed hysterically causing Megan to laugh hysterically. "Why are we laughing, Alice?"

Chapter 21

Abbottsford, Wisconsin—Charlie's parents' house.
35 years ago…

Alice stood at the kitchen sink, up to her elbows in suds and water—with a scouring pad in hand, scrubbing the pots and pans from the morning breakfast of ham and eggs, and home-baked yeast orange rolls. Charlie's mom, Alma, began rolling out the dough for pie. "I'm baking a cherry pie today. Do you like cherry pie, Alice?" Her voice whined like an accusation causing chills down Alice's back.

"I like blueberry the best, ma'am. I think cherry is my least favorite. In fact, I detest it. But I am sure your pie is very good."

"Well, I am making it because it's Charlie's favorite pie of all time. I have a special recipe that I will share with you because you will be expected to bake this for him once a week. No matter if you like cherry or not. That doesn't matter."

"How kind of you to share the recipe with me." Alice tried her best to be sweet and respectful like her mother taught her, even though her insides were churning with resentment.

On and on Alma chattered. This time it was about cleaning up behind Charlie. Pressing and ironing. Waiting on him. Putting Alice second made her wonder if any man in this family put his wife first. Alma felt women were to marry and keep the husband happy at all costs. If you followed the rules of keeping your weight under a certain poundage, which Alma considered to be one hundred twenty pounds, smile, never nag, and cook and clean and wait on him, he will be happy. Therefore, you will also be happy. There had to be justice in this world of inequality of marriage.

Alice sat down with a glass of iced tea, her mind feeling as if a window had cracked open allowing fresh air to blow through. But where was her happiness? Was she allowed any? What was Charlie's part in this relationship? What was his share in this marriage? The terms were clear. Concise. Somehow, she had inadvertently agreed to all of this when she stood at the altar and should have caught a clue when they were pronounced 'man and wife'—which meant he was the man of the place, and she was merely a wife—his wife. Staying with Charlie only made her bitter. The person Alice once was, vanished. Disappeared.

"Are you listening to me about this recipe?" Alma snapped, pulling Alice from her thoughts. "Alice?"

"Alice?"

****

Present day

"Alice? Alice? Alice, did you hear Megan? She asked if you wanted pie. Cherry pie sounds good to me." Simon scratched his collarbone.

Alice felt as though her insides blew as she stopped laughing. The anger began in her belly and flared outward through her arms and exploded in her head. "No, thanks. Cherry pie does not sound good. I hate cherry pie and I will never eat another piece of cherry pie as long as I live. Is that okay with everyone?"

Everyone looked around with wide eyes and quickly nodded. "Yes, it's okay with me too."

Simon took Alice's hand and shook it as though trying to awaken her from a nightmare. She yanked back and walked to the kitchen counter.

"What is your favorite pie, Megan?" It felt as though her eyes were popping from their sockets and the question she just asked was pressing.

"Why, I—" She pressed her hand to her chest.

"I am sure you have a favorite kind of pie. Simon, what is your favorite kind of pie?" She hurled around to face him as Fiona walked back in with the camera gear.

The dog barked, baring clean teeth.

Fiona did an about-face to walk back out when Alice yelled, "Stop right there. Fiona, tell us your favorite pie?"

"Ohm, Alice, really, this is your pressing question of the moment? Have you lost your mind? What does pie have to do with anything?"

"Everything. Pie has to do with everything. And everybody here. I just want to know what your favorite is so tell me. Don't you know how to answer a simple question?" Livid, she stomped her foot, and her heart picked up speed.

"Peach?" she mumbled as though she were afraid of giving the wrong response, all the while the large dog kept barking. "But if that's the wrong answer, I can pick a different fruit."

Alice turned around and pointed at Simon.

"Apple," he snapped.

"Blueberry," Megan hollered.

"Mine too! Oh, Megan, I love blueberry, but it

always had to be cherry pie just like everything else. I didn't matter. But I matter now, and you matter now and we want to eat blueberry pie."

Charlie sprang to his feet."Get the hell out of here, Alice. And take your people with you."

"Megan, if you are happy with Charlie then good for you. But, if I just described your life when I told you about mine, then leave. Come with us."

"Oh, I couldn't. I just couldn't." Megan stumbled backward.

Charlie charged across the room as Simon jumped up to bar his path to Alice.

Undeterred, Alice held her ground. Charlie looked her in the eye and stopped moving.

"This anger I feel is so liberating. I suddenly feel so free. I came looking for closure and I got it. I am no longer afraid of you, or the past, or what my parents told me about milk."

"Oh, I didn't know you were thirsty. May I get you a glass?" Megan asked innocently.

"I think that is our queue to leave." Simon took Fiona by one hand and grabbed Alice with the other, but Alice wouldn't budge. Her eyes were fixed on Charlie's wife.

"Megan, I'm asking you again. Is there any place you would like to go? Like to a relative, or friend? Or, home with me?"

"I hear there's a pullout bed," Fiona said. "Simon told me."

Megan shook her head and looked away. "I'm staying right here with my husband."

On the way to the car, Alice kept glancing back toward the cabin, hoping Megan would come—and then she did. She came running with a small suitcase in her hand.

"You can have the front seat, Alice," Fiona said, climbing into the back of the SUV. "You earned it."

Once Megan was safely in the back with Fiona, Alice jumped into the front. "And then there were four."She turned in the seat to see what Charlie was doing, but he was nowhere to be seen. The door was shut, but now here came the dog racing after the moving SUV.

Simon pulled to a stop and Megan opened her door. The dog jumped inside. Uncertain about the dog's temperament, she started to protest when the large animal crawled between the front captain chairs and sat on her lap. Alice leaned as far back as she could. "Megan?"

"Jasper is a sweetheart. Don't let him fool you."

"Oh good." Alice timidly began to stroke his ears.

"Want me to pull over and put him in the way back?" Simon asked.

"No, I think we are good." Alice was smashed against a ball of fluff on a seventy-pound dog probably trained to hate women by her ex.

"That was interesting." Simon smiled as he gunned down the road.

"Well, you sure got more than you bargained for with that little trip down memory lane, Alice," Fiona quipped. "If we pick up any more passengers on your forthcoming glimpses into the past, we'll need a bus to return home."

Alice laughed as her thoughts fluttered across the years. She sighed relieved; pleased she had made the right choice by leaving despite her 'parents' humiliation concerning her choice of divorce. Today her decision was validated and rid herself of guilt. Closure was checked off the list.

"What have I done?" Megan asked herself aloud.

"Do you want to go back?" Fiona asked.

"I don't know what I want to do. I will when I settle down a bit," Megan replied, rubbing her stomach. "Give me time. Meanwhile, I had this packed suitcase ready to visit my sister and just grabbed it."

"Pretend you're on a vacation with us." Fiona patted her leg. "One crabby gal is plenty. Not sure I could possibly cope with another."

They drove in silence for ten miles before Simon commented. "What do we do with that chapter in my book?"

"Maybe it won't be a chapter. Maybe that was just for me. And Megan."*And perhaps in my book.*

"Whatever you think best, honey."

Honey? Alice's spirit warmed.

Chapter 22

Alice

Something was terribly wrong. Her body wouldn't move. Last night she consumed an entire bottle of wine before bed while watching TV. If only she had shown more self-control but the effect of seeing Charlie again was too much to take without alcohol intervention.

There was a light tapping at the hotel door. Alice was barely awake, but her chest hurt terribly. It was nearly impossible to take in the air. It felt as though an elephant sat on her chest. Thank goodness she was still alive. Thank goodness they all were. Just hours earlier, she had run away from Charlie for the second time. Stress did horrible things to the body and mind. Certain she now was in the throes of a heart attack, she knew she needed help and tried to get up, but it was no use.

Slowly, she opened her eyes, suddenly feeling dizzy at the same time she felt the swipe of something long and wet on her face. She gagged and then realized it wasn't a heart attack. Nor was it an elephant. It was Jasper. He sat on her chest and looked down at her. Somehow, she managed to move him next to her on the double bed, where he quietly rolled over.

Rain battered against the windows; it was barely seven and still dark outside. Feet away, Fiona snored like a wild boar. Megan slept curled up on the small couch with a blanket flung over her. Poor woman, for now, there was no place for her but with them. Maybe when her spirit settled a bit, she'd decide what to do.

There was another tap on the door. Alice slid from bed and tip-toed across the room. Simon was already dressed.

"Are you all right?" he whispered.

"I am. There's a lot I need to mull over, yet, but I slept well."

"Mull it over with me for a while." He nodded toward the elevator. "Breakfast?"

"Sure. I need to get dressed first. What about the sleeping bear?"

He smiled at the snoring. "Let her and Megan sleep. I'll meet you downstairs."

"Give me thirty minutes to get ready. Oh, I need to take Jasper out first."

The long hot shower felt good pelting against her skin—it allowed her to release years of pent-up anger. It seemed to ooze from her pores and run down her legs, puddle about her ankles, and then empty out the drain. Up to this moment, she had carried the scars that were only visible on her soul, yet they ripped her confidence from time to time. It was time to release it all. Begin again. The shower was a baptism of sorts and new beginnings. She reveled in her newfound strength and courage. It also felt good to be helping Megan.

After the shower, she wrapped herself in a thick white bathrobe and leaned over the bathroom sink to take a good look at herself in the mirror. The overhead harsh lights revealed more facial lines than she remembered having yesterday. It was startling and she made a mental note to buy some of that expensive cream that instantly rubbed away wrinkles on the hands and face.

Shrugging it off, she blew dried her hair, and tucked away stragglers of her bound gray hair, a looped ponytail parading as a bun. She added a bit of makeup to her face, chose a pair of light gray jeans with a sleeveless shell top, flabby arms be damned—and slipped into her light jacket adorned with embroidery and tapestry. She loved the fanciful jacket with the out-of-style raglan sleeves—perfect for the Wyoming morning drop in temperature.

Alice used an old belt for the leash and looped it onto Jasper's collar. After their walk, she spotted Simon waiting at a small table, big enough for two, no more. If Fiona woke up and saw them, she would be forced to sit elsewhere. No room for her. No room for Megan. Just room for Simon and Alice.

"Excuse me, but you cannot take the dog into the dining room." The receptionist stopped her.

"Oh, this is a seeing-eye dog." Alice lied.

"You don't appear to be blind."

"Not me, him." She pointed toward Simon who was staring off into the distance.

"Okay."

Alice sat down opposite Simon with Jasper quietly under her feet.

"I held your place with a glass of orange juice." He smiled while a look of fondness held her gaze. "Your hair smells of green apple. Shampoo?"

"Yes. Just got off the phone with Talia." She shook the folded napkin and placed it on her lap.

"How's the baby room coming along?"

"She hasn't seen Zeba in days. That's of great

concern to me. I left my daughter a message to return my call. So far, she hasn't."

"Oh boy."

"Yeah, 'oh boy'. The problem with Zeba is that she desires monetary rewards. Me too. But I expect them because I work for them. My daughter would rather I hand her what I have earned. And usually, she gets her way, sorry to say. My fault. If I can't reach her by tomorrow, I may have to book a flight to Dallas. I know it's not what you want to hear."

"Don't fret, it'll turn out fine. Right now, I'm worried about you. How are you doing after seeing Charlie? Talk to me."

"Yesterday was hard on many levels, but today I feel set free."

"Really? Well, that's good news." He spoke as though he wasn't so sure it was true. "Maybe the wine I bought you last night has something to do with it."

"I have stuffed down the past for so long, refusing to deal with it. I think a part of me shut down." She sipped her orange juice.

"And now, are you dealing with it?"

"Dealt with it. I faced it yesterday. I just wish I hadn't taken so long to release the nightmare."

"Hold it right there. I'll be right back." Simon got up from the table and returned with a plate of French toast with syrup and real butter. "I know this is your favorite breakfast. My treat."

"Of course it is. It comes with the room." She winked at the receptionist who now scowled at them. "And my favorite breakfast makes my jeans too tight. Today, I do not care. Tomorrow might be another story." She laughed digging into the meal, fully thankful for Simon's attention.

"Stop being so hard on yourself. Everyone is always striving to improve; cook healthier, take a class, and lose four pounds."

"Twenty." Alice leaned forward. "Here's the trick life hands you. You think everything will work out for the best, and then it doesn't. So far, this trip has been enlightening."

"I knew it would." He winked.

"Next summer, let's tip-toe through your tulips, and I will be the one standing around taking pictures."

"Let's finish this road trip first before we start contemplating the next." Simon took a sip of coffee. "I should have helped you more back then with Charlie; Thomas too."

"You helped plenty. Want me to tell you a secret?"

Simon smiled. "Yes. I just didn't know we kept secrets from each other."

"Here's one. If you had come to my wedding, I would not have married Charlie." She shoved a fork full of French toast, slathered with butter and dripping with maple syrup, into her mouth.

"How so?"

"Standing at the altar, I looked for you." She shoved her resurfacing feelings for Simon down with another piece of food.

"Me? But you were marrying Charlie. How did I matter?"

"I never really had gotten over you—from you know, before, that fling we had in Corpus? If you had walked into the church on my wedding day, well, I might have left with you." Her breath tangled in her chest.

"I'm speechless."

"The things I thought about while putting on my wedding dress that day. Here I had been dreaming of and planning for my wedding day, and then it finally comes, and who am I thinking about? Not my husband-to-be."

"Alice." He looked sad.

"Oh, forget it. Anyway, you helped me plenty when Zeba was small and I left Thomas, marriage number one and two."

He looked oddly at her.

"What?"

"Nothing. I just hope I didn't push you too hard about this trip."

Alice set down her fork and laughed as she signaled to the waitress. "Now you say that! When we are a thousand miles from home! Good timing."

"What can I get for you?" the waitress asked.

"A very tall glass of a mimosa."

Chapter 23

Simon
On the road

"Packed and ready to move forward. Where to?" Simon asked of the women as he fiddled with the radio in the driver's seat. Megan and Fiona sat in the back while Alice and Jasper snagged the front.

The women remained quiet.

"Silence? I am in this vehicle with three women and there is nothing but silence. Mute women cannot be a good thing. What are you all plotting?" He needed to find something to break the icy stillness. "Okay, I will start. I am thinking about going from point A, which is where we are—in front of this hotel, to point B which is, where? Ladies?"

"I guess that decision is Alice's." Fiona tapped her on the shoulder. "Go."

Simon looked over and spotted the hurt in Alice. "A penny for your thoughts."

"I should call Zeba, and touch base with Talia before the days done." She dug through her purse and pulled out an aspirin bottle.

He turned toward the back. "Megan, are you doing, okay?"

"I'm thinking about Charlie."

"Then she's not doing okay." Alice lifted her brow

while swallowing the tablets.

"Do you miss him?" Fiona asked.

"Wondering what I should do."

"Well, I know what you are not doing and that is going back to him," Alice said softly.

"Listen, lady, I'm an adult and do not need you, or Charlie, or anyone else telling me what I am or what I am not going to do, hear me?"

Alice nodded and rubbed her forehead. "Okay, okay. Just trying to give a little help here. You need not be so touchy."

"I need to decompress and think my own thoughts." Megan buckled her seat belt.

"Well, since we know what Megan is thinking, I am thinking about having fun. How about you, Simon?" Fiona asked. "Are ya up for fun?"

"I'm up for fun. I'll program my GPS for it."

"Alice, are you up for fun, too? What are you thinking about?" Fiona asked.

"I am thinking about Tupperware." She stared out the window.

"Tupperware?" Simon laughed.

"Yes, you see, before I married Charlie, I was thrown a Tupperware shower. I received every type of Tupperware that ever had been made. Boxes and boxes of it; storage containers in every size with lids, tumblers, jello-ring molds, citrus peelers—"

"Oh, I just love those orange citrus peelers," Fiona interjected. "I lost mine. Do you happen to still have yours? If so, may I have it?"

"Bowls, popsicle molds, salt and pepper shakers, ketchup and mustard containers, measuring cup and spoon sets, colander and stocking canisters, just to name a few. All in Harvest Gold, Avocado Green and Orange-Orange," Alice continued in a trance-like state of mind.

"Are you okay?" Simon gently took her hand.

"I should have skipped going to that shower and gone to Colorado instead."

"Colorado?" Simon asked.

"Because I've never been. That day, I had this sudden urge to see the mountains. If I had gone, I would never have married Charlie. I just know this."

"I thought you wouldn't have married Charlie if I had shown up at the wedding?"

"That too."

Simon set the GPS, started the SUV, and pulled out in traffic.

"Where are we going?" Fiona asked.

"Somewhere fun to toss snowballs for you, Fiona, and find the mountains of Colorado for Alice."

Chapter 24

Simon

It was two o'clock beneath a colorless sky in the afternoon of the following day when Simon pulled off onto a remote slippery road. Alice, Fiona, and Megan quickly popped open their car doors and stepped out of the vehicle and onto the postcard charm of the snowy mountains. Simon reached for his backpack and pulled out the camera. Whatever the women did, he'd catch it all.

While the women explored the small area, Simon sighed with relief. For now, it seemed they were taking a break from bickering. It was frustrating to listen to them harp on each other. More than once he was tempted to take them all back home. It was nearly impossible to negotiate peace between them. Yet, each woman had such a unique essence about them. Why couldn't they tap into that? Why didn't they see a commonality to build a friendship?

Born in different decades, Simon was surprised to find their important relationships had unhappy endings. Alice in her fifties, the oldest, twice divorced. Megan, in her mid-forties, about to leave her husband—or not. Fiona, the youngest, a widow, barely thirty. They have much in common; heartbreak, pain, and disappointment in the love they found, or didn't find.

Alice could have a meltdown by meeting her past. He needed to be sure he was there for her. Megan, the stranger and wild factor. What would she decide? Stay or leave an abusive relationship? Is it possible to mend it? There was and then, what about Fiona, who lost her newlywed husband, but still tried to bring peace to the lives of the volatile forces of Megan's snippiness and Alice's bluntness? Three remarkable women who shared immeasurable suffering but had trouble connecting with one another. It was then a new idea perked. As observed the women he realized it wasn't just about Alice anymore. And would his publisher approve? He was contracted and paid, and now wants to change the theme? Simon swallowed hard. It was worth a chance.

Simon stopped for a moment at the rear of the vehicle and breathed in scents of cold and pine—refreshing after months of penetrating heat. Snow-filled trees surrounded them, their branches weighed down by clumps of snow and the falling snowflakes growing thicker. The snow fell like confetti as a cardinal made a startled movement and disappeared into the white forest, lamenting the cool shot he just missed.

He leaned against the car's hood, hunching his shoulders around his neck, and watched the women toss snowballs at each other while Jasper ran his nose along the ground, making a ribbon trail.

"Hey, let's build a snowman and use some of these." Reaching for pinecones, Alice swept branches of overhanging trees, causing snow to tumble down on her head. "Ah! I am freezing cold and wet!"

Simon dug through the trunk and grabbed a light jacket, now wishing he had chosen one heavier. The bottom of his pants was soaked along with his socks and shoes that needed to be changed, but he didn't think about that. Instead, he held out the jacket for Alice to slip into, then zipped it to her chin.

"Thanks." She smiled and did a half courtesy before turning her attention to creating a snowman.

"Wait." Simon held her arm to keep her in place. Did she almost kiss him?

"What?" She smiled; her cheeks so red with cold that she seemed so irresistible. He wanted to kiss her but then saw Megan and Fiona watching them.

"What?" Alice repeated.

"Nothing. You just look cold, is all." Simon held up his camera as she trotted off to rejoin the others.

By now, dozens of shots were taken with his camera. Panning through them, he noticed most of the pictures were of Alice. How could they not be? She was tall, and her limbs moved loosely as she navigated the cold. She wore jeans, a blouse, and now his jacket— sleeves too long for her arms. The bangles on her wrist played music with each movement. On her feet were soaked tennis shoes. Her large, round eyes were lit with happiness and joy over the moment. She pulled the collar around her neck, and her curly hair was wound into a bun. For now, her face appeared carefree and—so appealing. Playful, solid, and familiar. His gaze lingered over her face. It seemed an eternity since he had truly looked at her. Everything changed in that moment. He wanted to hold her and ask forgiveness for the past. *How did I ever let you go?*

Simon returned his camera to the car and took out Fiona's instamatic. As he snapped additional shots of the three women, he focused on Alice the most, recalling the young woman who came with him to a Texas beach; how good it felt walking beside her, and how sexy the two-piece swimsuit looked riding low on her skinny hips. She smiled a lot in those days. It was the most carefree smile he had ever seen. Alice still wore that same smile from time to time. Worry shaved some of that away. Being so close to her proved to be challenging at times. Over the years there were periods impossible not to think about her romantically. It reminded him of the hurt and the mistake he made when he left.

A smack of a snowball hit his shoulder bringing him out of his thoughts. "Hey, watch the camera, would you?" Simon called jovially above the increasing wind.

Now Alice held very still watching him. As if waiting to tell her something. Why was it that words were lost in person, but somehow always managed to find them on paper? Long ago she knocked on the door to his life, and he invited her in, and it never was the same. At least not for him.

Simon caught sight of the snowman. It stood there, immovable, facing the road, bathed in cold, surrounded by the women preening him. It seemed to be smiling. Then he took the last picture of the day. The three women had gathered around it, arms joined, making the snowman a part of their entourage.

A snowplow carefully steered down the way and pulled to a stop at the curve. The driver rolled down his window and leaned out.

"Can you believe it's June and here we are in snow?" Fiona's voice was falsetto with excitement.

"We can get snow through the end of the month. You might want to drive on behind me. This is my last pass, and you don't want to be stuck up here."

Simon waved at him, and the woman ran back to the SUV with Jasper following. "I don't know about you ladies, but I am ready to head for warmer weather."

"Just be careful going down the mountain. There is plenty of ice under that snow." The snowplow began its descent down the mountain.

Alice turned the heater to high. "Thanks, Simon, for taking me to Colorado. It took years but I finally made it."

The further down they went, the warmer the air and the less snow they saw until there were just patches left here and there on either side of the road. On the radio old country songs played.

Simon hummed.

"I believe that is the first time I have ever heard you hum. That's an excellent hum you have there."

"Hey, Alice."

"Yes, Megan."

"I didn't want to tell you this earlier, but I think we have your Tupperware back at the cabin."

Chapter 25

Megan

The women shared a room in a log-cabin-like
motel along the roadside, deep in the shadow of
evening. Never mind that it was summer. The
mountains made it feel more like winter.

Megan crossed the room, self-conscious of her thin
frame beneath her borrowed nightgown. Fiona was
tolerable. It was impossible not to like her. But what
held Megan's attention and curiosity was Alice—due to
the fact she was her husband's ex—and his first wife.
She couldn't help but compare herself. Alice was older
than she, but no more than ten years, about Charlie's
age. Alice's small bosoms accentuated her waist. The
shape of her legs and thighs, and the graceful curve of
her neck were attractive. Charlie's ex-wife was quite
pretty but somehow still broken, even after all these
years. It made her ponder if Alice was broken since
childhood, or if several men had worn her down over
the decades.

Lost in thought, the fortyish woman sat on the bed,
taking items from her purse, examining them for their
usefulness, and then either trashing them, or placing
them into her save pile. Eyeliner, coins, coupons were
saved; receipts, and empty gun wrappers, trashed. She
checked her phone for messages. Darn. It was dead. She

got out her cord and plugged in her cell. Now she couldn't talk to Charlie even if she wanted to. A ride of emotions tumbled through her spirit. Megan sighed needing some way to make sense of it all; her loyalty to her husband and her unexpected bolt from him into the arms of strangers. "I think I need to talk. Sort things out."

Alice ended her call to Stella and sat beside Megan. "Sorry for what I said the other day about Charlie. I want you to know, we are all here for you— Simon, Fiona, and me."

Not liking her close proximity to the woman once married to her husband, Megan moved down a bit. She needed space. Jasper was in bed behind her, covered up and with a pillow beneath his head.

"Jasper is a darling." Alice stroked him. "A great dog. Very gentle."

"He's my baby." Megan wanted Alice to know he still belonged to her.

"Did you and Charlie want children? I'm sorry, that's too personal."

"I don't mind answering. Sure, we wanted them. It just never happened. How about you?"

"Just one. Second marriage."

"I bet you have a million thoughts reeling through your mind, after yesterday," Fiona said.

"I do have some."

"I'm ready to listen to each one."

"You aren't alone," Alice said. "When I went through my divorce, I kept asking myself hard questions. Was I predestined for this life? For this marriage? Were the choices mine to make, or was my path laid out before me at birth? Am I the selfish one needing freedom? And if it's really up to me, what direction do I want to take right now?"

"Deep, Alice. You are such a sage." Fiona rattled through her makeup bag and looked in the mirror at the women behind her. "I'm all ears when you're ready to unburden, Megan."

"Put yourselves in my shoes," Megan said, winding her fingers through the bare spot of the bedspread. "All my life, up until the time I met Charlie, I've dedicated myself to living my life alone, for me."

"Such as?" Fiona dabbed her face with an astringent.

"Since I thought I'd never marry, I had long-term and short-term goals. Buying a house was a long-term goal. Money in the bank a short-term. Then I met Charlie. He just swept me off my feet. There aren't many men who want to marry an older woman."

"You can't be older than Charlie," Alice said.

"Of course not. I'm ten years younger. I mean, men want the younger ones—the *way* younger ones—just a day over legal age if at all possible. It impressed me that he didn't go for a twenty-year-old. He wanted someone closer to his own age. Me."

"You had money saved."

"Not nice, Alice!" Fiona shushed.

There was a pause. A very long pause. After a deep breath, Megan said, "I had a domineering dad, so when Charlie came along, it seemed familiar. It's what I had been doing all my life; being ruled by a man which isn't necessarily a bad thing. I like a take-charge man."

"It's calming to have a loving and gentle man watching over you," Fiona pointed out. "I had one. Maybe one day I will find that again, but not counting on it."

"Again? What happened to him? Are you still in touch?" Megan asked.

"Not unless I hire a medium to contact him. He passed, not long ago." Tears welled up in her eyes.

"Oh, I am so sorry."

Fiona nodded. "I am thinking about contacting him when I get back to NOLA after just to check on him to be sure he is alright and all."

Megan watched Fiona turn away trying to hide her tears. "It's normal to cry. You are safe here."

Fiona slid into a chair.

"Fiona was blessed with a good one. Not like us who found an abusive man," Alice sputtered."I don't mean that as an insult, Fiona, but, Megan—sometimes we, as women, become used to being treated a certain way by men, that we become acclimated to it, and lose sight of what is normal. It sounds as though your dad might have been controlling."

"I get what you are saying." Megan wondered if Alice was revealing a confidence about herself.

"You are free now. I went through years of counseling—well, a few. I highly recommend it. We just make the most of what life deals us and move forward."

"Move forward to where?" Megan sharply responded, enunciating each word as if they were arrows.

Just then they heard Simon pound on the wall from the next room. "Stop arguing."

They all answered at once, "OK."

"From being controlled by a lunatic to being free and making your own choices," Alice lowered her voice. "I know what your life has been like. I left Charlie too, remember?"

"Alice, do you have a single unspoken thought?" Fiona whispered.

Judged by a woman she didn't care much for, Megan blasted Alice. "Yes, I do. How can I forget when you keep mentioning it every two seconds? And if I remember correctly, you also left your next husband. You have relationship issues so please wipe that judgmental look off your face." Megan felt ready to denounce Alice when Fiona's voice broke through the heated exchange.

"You might want to skip that part in moving forward," Fiona lightly suggested to Megan.

"You know it's just a matter of time until Charlie comes for you."

Megan wasn't so sure that would be a bad thing.

"When that happens, don't be scared. He will try to scare you. It's going to be a rough road for a while, but millions of people manage it. You can too. I will help you."

"Megan, you deserve to feel loved and beautiful." Fiona patted her hand.

"I am loved," Megan answered.

Fiona smiled. "Of course you are."

"Charlie loves me."

"Well, I give up." Alice walked to the windows and parted the curtains.

Megan hated Alice's arrogance and thinking she knew everything about her life with Charlie. "The whole thing is like a movie on television that I cannot turn off. I woke up this morning forgetting what happened. When I didn't find Charlie beside me, I thought he left early for work."

"He never did anything early—well maybe one thing." Alice smirked, still peering outside.

"Alice. Again, do you have a single unspoken thought?"

"You know what I think, Alice?" Megan said. "I think you are still carrying a torch for him so you can get back with him."

"Now you have gone crazy just like Charlie," Alice hollered.

Another knock on the wall.

"Look, you just left the man. Give yourself time to acclimate." Alice's tone softened.

Megan clenched her fist in frustration. Never had she felt so confused. The feeling of triumph the day she left Charlie had passed. She knew that this was not a breakthrough in leaving her husband, although she had considered it at least a half dozen times. Now she felt like a minor character in a puppet show with Alice pulling her strings. Running away from Charlie had been simple. Everything else was complicated. "Alice, did you love Charlie when you left him?"

Alice shook her head.

"But I still love him." Tears stung her eyes. "What do I do with that?"

Alice shook her head again. "When I married Charlie, he didn't know what love was. I thought if I showed him what it was, if I gave it to him, then he would open and flourish—we would flourish. But it never happened. I withered and died."

"That's the difference between us. Charlie loves me, it's obvious he didn't love you." A life with Charlie was hard. A life without him impossible. Megan felt her heart pound faster in her chest."I miss my home."

"I noticed you aren't wearing your wedding ring," Fiona commented.

"It has nothing to do with anything. I took it off to wash my hands when preparing your snack plate the other day." She looked down at her finger, feeling contempt over being put on the spot. Didn't she have a right to love whom she loved, and live the way she wanted? Why did she feel she needed these women's validation? She hated herself for needing approval.

Escaping Charlie seemed like the right thing to do at the time. It was a knee-jerk reaction due to the argument they had the evening before when he got the phone call about Alice and her entourage arriving for an interview of sorts, to say nothing of the tension in the air when they arrived. He had hurt her so many times; not so much physically, but the words he used were crushing. The cherry pie conversation did her in. Now, all she could think about were the good times. Most of all, she felt sorry for him, sitting in the cabin all alone. Most likely he was remorseful by now, she hoped. Megan went to the bathroom and re-emerged minutes later fully dressed.

Alice exchanged a confused look with Fiona. "Where are you going?"

"I'm hungry. I'm going for a snack." Megan grabbed her cell and purse.

"Want company?" Alice asked, getting to her feet.

"No. I need space from you both. Keep an eye on Jasper?" The last thing she wanted was Alice trailing along behind, continuing the exhausting conversation. Out of sight from the women's prying eyes, Megan felt as much relief being away from them as she was being away from Charlie. Across the street was an all-night café where she sat staring at the menu. After ordering a hamburger and fries, she pulled her cell out and checked for messages. Her heart flipped. All ten calls were from Charlie.

"Where the hell are you? Get your ass back home now."

Her heart hardened. *How dare you talk to me like that?*

"If you don't come home now, I promise to hunt you down and don't think that I won't."

Fear encompassed her. *Where can I go to escape?*

"Did you know you left dirty dishes for me to clean up?"

Anger welled. *Do them yourself.*

"Damn you, Megan, where are my fresh shirts? They better be ironed when I find them."

Panic set in. *I can't remember where I put them. Are they even washed?*

The messages took a calmer turn. "Hey, Megan, if you need a vacation go ahead and take it, but don't leave me. I love you."

Tension eased. *I knew it.*

"Sweet Megan, please call me. I so would love to hear your voice."

Her heart melted. *Charlie.*

"Guess what I bought for you today. A gazebo! Yes, I know it was expensive, but you always wanted one. I am going to have it built several yards from the house so you can plant your garden around it."

She became happy. *See, Alice, he does the sweetest things for me.*

"Honey, when do you think you will be coming

home? It's sure lonesome without you."

Suddenly she felt lonely for him. *I miss you too.*

"I love you, sugar."

Love welled toward him.

"Megan, I can't live without you. I will go to counseling with you if that's what it takes. And damn that Jasper for deserting me too."

She chuckled. *Yes, counseling will solve it all.*

Megan ate slowly, as though each bite were a new thought to consider.

Her mind drifted to their whirlwind courtship days. Their first date was when Charlie took her to the County Fair. He tried but didn't win any stuffed animals for her, which only resulted in her laughing because time and again he missed looping the ring around any of the small objects.

"I think those critters are jeering at me. And I hope you are laughing with me and not at me."

"I'd never laugh at you, but I will stop laughing if you tell me to."

"Stop laughing." A goofy smile spread across his lips.

"Oh, Charlie." She rubbed his arm. "I'm too old for any stuffed animal anyway. Let's get an elephant ear to eat instead, okay? My treat."

"An elephant ear? Those things are big!" he told her as they walked toward the food stand.

By evening's end, they had gone on nearly all the rides. Charlie felt the effects of them combined with beer. The couple walked slowly, hand in hand, to the car where he kissed her for the first time, sending chills clear down to the bottom of her toes. A month later, Charlie was hired as a ranger in Wyoming. So afraid she would never see him again, she felt a rush of relief when he asked her to marry him. He even got down on his knee and held out a nice ring—the most romantic act she ever experienced. So what if the ring was cubic zirconia. After a quickie church wedding, they packed the car and made their way west to a new life.

Things only got bad between them if he didn't have a good day at work. The public that he dealt with could be demanding and didn't like to follow the park rules. Charlie didn't have patience for dealing with the tourists and he needed some relief. No, she didn't like when he pouted or ranted or blamed her ineptness as a wife as the root of his problems. She'd wait till he sorted out his anger and realized that she was for him and not against him. Megan tried to let him know that every day. Some days it seemed to sink in while other days he didn't seem to care.

Megan yawned and looked at the clock above the restaurant counter. It was early morning—nearly daylight. The real truth of the matter was, she felt alive, and free. For now, she would relish the sensation, unconcerned of where today would lead. Then she took out a scratch paper from her purse along with an ink pen and drew a line down the center. On one side she wrote all the things about him that were good and on the other, all the bad things. She remained until dawn mulling it over, just as a bus heading east rolled up in front.

Chapter 26

Alice

Alice woke by a sound and lifted the brown flowered spread from off her face. At least she thought there had been a sound. Like a closing door. But she must have been wrong, perhaps dreaming. A white rectangle of moonlight extended across the floor from the window. The numbers on the digital clock were lit up: 5:14. She shut her eyes, willing sleep to return. Fragments of images floated through her mind, a jumble of memories tied to Simon—their walks in the park, his gentle words, and the warmth she felt whenever they were together. Why did they constantly go there into no-man's-land where they did her no good? She wondered if he ever thought of her in the same way. The secret of how she felt about Simon sat in her mouth for so long that it had grown quite comfortable there.

Only feet away, she yearned to walk the few feet to the door and go to him in his room, drop her nightgown in the dark drawn curtain room, and crawl beneath the blankets. When he turned in sleep and awoke to find her, how would he react? She pressed her eyelids closed and thought of him reaching for her. Running his hands down the length of her body, moving his body closer, kissing her neck. If they made love, the rest of the trip might become awkward. Would they become a couple? Would he withdraw? Or become embarrassed because of Fiona and Megan? If he turned her away, she couldn't bear the rest of the trip. It'd turn into her ultimate rejection. Their friendship would be over, forever, once more. And just how did Fiona figure into all of this? Was she chasing Simon as a replacement for her late husband? And just what happened between them in New Orleans that extra month he stayed after meeting her?

She opened her eyes and turned in bed to see Fiona sound asleep wearing the same clothes from the night before and wondered how anyone could fall asleep without a shower and clean pajamas.

Jasper sat up and looked at Alice, pleadingly whining to go outside. She narrowed her eyes at the dog who had slept on the pull-out sofa bed, but where was Megan? Alice sat up on her elbows to get a better look. The bathroom door was open, lights out. Had she returned from getting a snack last night? Worry crowded her mind. Perhaps she had pushed the woman too hard during their conversation right back into the arms of her husband.

Surely, if Megan left for good, she'd take her dog, right? Alice got out of bed and parted the curtains. The start of the day looked dreary and overcast. A few people ambled through the parking lot. Reflecting on their recent conversations, Alice decided to be kinder. After all, Megan had been through a lot. Of all people, Alice understood. It was like coming out of battle into safety.

The sound of the doorknob rattling drew her attention. With a creak of the door, stood Megan, looking downcast and weary.

"Is everything okay?" Alice took a step toward her. "Where have you been? No, you don't have to answer that. It's just I woke up and you weren't here. I was worried."

Megan leaned her head against the wall and inhaled through her nose. "I had a lot of thinking to do."

"Well, you are here now. And safe." Alice felt edgy like she always did when something was going wrong; the unpredictability of someone whom she didn't know that well. "You must be exhausted."

"I am." Megan slid onto the couch next to Jasper.

"Perhaps, when you get settled, you could see someone; a professional to help you sort out your thoughts and feelings."

Megan stopped stroking Jasper. "Really?"

"I saw someone once. A long time ago. It didn't work out for me though. The therapist was younger than me. Seemed to have a different value system. I think he found me too, too…" Alice searched for the right word as her fingers fiddled with the sleeves of her nightgown.

"Pushy?"

"Boring."

"You don't project a dull image. You're vibrant, so self-assured."

"It's a façade. Listen, Megan, I am afraid we got off to a wrong start. My fault."

"I don't dislike you."

"But—I make you uncomfortable?"

Megan half shrugged. "You walked out on Charlie. It took him a while to get over you. A long while he loved you."

"It's called obsession."

"I checked my cell when I went to the burger place across from here. My phone was filled with his messages; from threatening to cajoling."

"How does that make you feel?" Alice didn't want to interject so much of her perspective in order to allow Megan to feel free to speak hers.

"Confused. Torn. He wants me back. And yet, I remain jealous of you."

"Now I'm confused." Alice sat across from her on the edge of the bed.

"You were his first wife. I am an afterthought. A substitute for who he really wants—you."

"That's not true." Alice felt shocked by Megan's words.

"I knew who you and Simon were the moment he opened the door."

"Oh?"

"Charlie reads Simon's weekly blog and shows special interest when it's about you."

"I had no idea."Alice was caught completely off guard. Charlie still stalked her.

"It always puts him into a very bad mood. I cannot compete."

"Megan, listen, you don't have to. And you don't have to define yourself by a man."

Alice reached for her hand, but Megan drew back.

"Speaking of dates," Megan said softly, "do you know which was my favorite? And yes, I read the column too."

"Tell me."

"It was a prearranged date, set for cocktails at a

local Denton place. Can't remember the name. The man owned a pool and spa business in another town. In the article, he seemed several years older than you. Can't remember if it was stated, or if it was an impression."

"Go on."

"He complained about women wanting to be with their girlfriends, or their children, or grandchildren, and then demanded to know where the boyfriend fitted in. He was arrogant, rich, and rude."

Alice searched her brain and momentarily couldn't remember this particular meeting; there had been so many. "Why was that one so much different than the others?"

"You stood up to him. You finished your drink, then said that you were going to the restroom and when you came out, you would leave. Alice Rigby was strong, determined, and her own woman in that moment."

"Don't you see the connection between what I did and you?" Alice paused before continuing. "I need to apologize to you. Sometimes I get so fired up about something, I want everyone to feel the same way I do. That's how I've treated you and I was wrong. Please forgive me."

"That was lovely. Thank you, Alice. Your words mean a lot. I've defended Charlie for so long, I'm not sure how to stop. I just wanted to make my marriage work."

"And now?" Alice watched the inflection of her voice, keeping it soft and even—without judgement.

"And now, I'm not sure what I want or where I belong. My emotions are all over the place."

"I do understand. I'm here if you feel like talking it

out, and I promise I will be kinder."

"Thanks."

"Wow, Alice, that was amazing. You have grown," Fiona said, from beneath the spread of her blankets.

Chapter 27

Alice
Wisconsin

The Wisconsin landscape was even lovelier than she remembered—lush and with myriads of colors in green; lime, avocado, jade, emerald—foliage so heavy it made it impossible to see further than a few feet into the undergrowth. Every leaf, each tree, even the clouds seemed to welcome her home. It was almost like knowing herself for the first time in a long time. The air seeped into her pores, and she felt warmed by the sun streaming through the car windows.

"I didn't realize how much I missed Wisconsin, until today."

"It's really beautiful, Alice," Megan said. "And houses are spread out, barns too. Just like Wyoming."

"I think Wyoming is even more spread out." Alice smiled, hoping for a nice visit with her parents.

They drove past a deserted property with only the foundation of an old house. An errant memory of her and her mother returned. Most Sundays found them driving through the country in search of deserted houses. One in particular remained vividly in her mind. This house was quite weather-beaten with a descript barn outback and a rusty swing set in the front yard surrounded by acres of wild chicory and Queen Anne's lace. Carefully, they tip-toed on rotted wood floorboards, looking out the windows that once held glass, framed in remnants of old lace curtains. Alice sighed with warm memories of telling her mom how she would renovate it. Is that where her love of design and desire for old houses began? How she wished Zeba was here to share this experience with her. To show her daughter where she went to school, where she grew up, and to see her grandparents again.

The call to her daughter went straight to voicemail. Not reaching her had now become more frightening than irritating. Next, she called Stella. It was bad news. Zeba and Martin weren't getting along, and the situation was getting in the way of her responsibilities, leaving it to Stella to pick up the slack. Worst of all, Talia's baby room design had been abandoned. "I would come immediately home, but I am on my way to my parents. It's their anniversary," Alice explained.

Stella went on to say that she still had it all under control just the same. Perhaps her mother might know more. Which sounded rather cryptic.

With the reference to her mother, Alice found herself missing her. Many times, they had been at odds, but Evelyn May Plunkett served as the voice of reason more often than not, that is, until she got her divorce when she told her to stick it out and make the best of it, and that cow and milk silliness concerning premarital sex. But she said it in her calm, controlled, and confident voice as though the short cliché advice was the right choice.

Evelyn was regal and carried herself with grace, taking long strides, head up, and always wore makeup, and a freshly pressed dress. There was an ease about her of sincere warmth although there always seemed to be a challenge of some sort between them brewing like what to wear, who not to date, and do not move to Texas under any circumstances. Something about the heat would do her in.

Alice was returning home after many years away. It meant she would be in good, safe hands for a few days. The food would be exceptionally delicious, the bed linens fresh, the lawn perfectly manicured, and everything would be in its place. Right now, Alice needed order.

And just as she knew to expect, Evelyn watched out the window. When the SUV pulled into the circular drive, her mother was out the door, hurrying toward her with arms open wide. Like a child, Alice allowed herself to be wrapped up in them, as she lay her head on her mother's shoulder. Suddenly, she felt safe and that everything would be okay.

"Mom."

"My Alice. Welcome home."

The reunion became perfect when her dad wrapped his arms around them both. "Welcome home, pumpkin."

"Thanks, Dad."

Alice made the introductions and soon they gathered around the table having dinner, chatting as old friends.

Nearing the 4th of July and her parents' sixtieth wedding anniversary, Alice felt content in the log cabin, whose windows faced Lake Delavan. Alice slept in her old room and Simon, along with the ladies, stayed in their guest house.

In the morning, Alice was just getting out of bed,

when her mother tapped at her door. "Can we talk?"

"Of course." Alice patted the bed beside her.

"I heard from Zeba."

"Thank goodness. I've been trying to reach her for the better part of a week. How is she? What's happening?"

"It seems she and Martin have broken off the engagement. Is that good news, or not?" Evelyn folded her hands into her lap.

"I-I am not sure."Alice reached for her cell.

"Don't, dear. She wants alone time. She just wants you to know she is fine. She'll call you when she's ready to talk."

"Why did she call you instead of me?" Alice felt shunned.

"Perhaps because it's easier to speak to someone she isn't so close to than to someone she is close to. As mothers, we want to dash in and make everything okay, but we need to wait until our daughters make the move toward us. Otherwise, we come across as pushy and perhaps, a bit pejorative as I did with you."

Alice returned the cell to the bedside table.

Evelyn continued. "If I could go back to those days, I would have given you exactly what you needed—a safe place to live—here. Most of all, I would have kept my mouth shut. We learn as we go along. I have regret."

"Mom, I love you so much." Alice hugged her tightly.

"Alice, I love you too. And as for Zeba, she will find her way, as you have."

"Well, in the meantime, we have an anniversary to plan for." Alice squeezed her mother's hand.

The day of the anniversary party, Alice stretched out in the shade on a lounger, wearing a modest one-piece bathing suit and reading Simon's latest column. Jasper stretched out on the grass beside her. If she voiced her opinion, the dog was much more bonded to her than Megan. Of course, she'd keep that opinion to herself. The sun shifted and began to edge its way up her legs. Not wanting to burn, Alice got to her feet to go inside, just as she noticed a man walk toward her.

Without warning, he picked her up and spun her about. She screamed. When he set her back on her feet, the six-footer smiled down at her. "Little Annie Swartz. I'd know you anywhere."

"Evidently not. I'm Alice. Alice Rigby."

"Are you sure?" He narrowed his eyes at her.

"My parents live right over there. They will vouch for me."

"Do you know an Annie Plunkett then?"

"No, name isn't familiar. Sorry."

"Is there going to be an anniversary party tonight?"

A bit alarmed, Alice didn't want to give out added information. "Why are you asking? And who are you?"

"I'm Alex Godfrey."

"Alice!"

Alice turned to see her mother calling to her from the portico. "Yes, Mother?"

"Gather your friends. I've made sandwiches."

"We'll be right up." Alice turned back to the stranger only to see him walk away.

The anniversary party was held at the yacht Club with live dance music. Her mother looked stunning in her silver dress. When she danced it was like moonlight in motion on water. Alice was thankful she was able to fit into one of her prom dresses. It was pink with layers of tulle. So what if she had to safety pin it closed in the back? The shawl covered it up nicely, if she only remembered to keep it in place. And Simon looked stunning in his jeans and white shirt and the dress jacket his dad lent him.

Just after ten, Alice noticed the man from earlier in the day speaking with Megan. What was his name? Alex Godfrey. That was it. Where did he fit? A bit leery of his presence, Alice decided to ask her mother about him, but just as she started across the dance floor, someone grabbed a hold of her and whirled her about before stumbling. "Hey, don't look frightened. It's me, Sam. I am about out of breath. Let's sit down."

"Sam." Alice threw her arms around him and held tightly to him. From the corner of her eye, she caught Simon with the camera. *He never stops working.*

Sam pulled her outside to the deck where they found a couple of seats.

"Sam, it's so good to see you. It's been way too long. How are you feeling?" Alice did her best to hide her surprise over his diminished appearance. His physical decline was obvious. How he managed to even make it to the celebration was baffling.

"Good days and bad. My prognosis isn't good, as you know. I might have a month on the calendar left."

"But you look so good." Alice's eyes welled up with tears.

"I'm glad you think so. But this cancer has taken its toll. I'm ready."

Alice wanted to ask how anyone could be ready for death but refrained. "I cannot imagine you being gone from my life."

"I'll never be far from you." He reached into his pocket and pulled out a half-dollar coin.

"What's this?"

"A wish to build a dream on. By the look on your face, I can tell you don't remember."

"Tell me." She took his hand.

"I'll let you remember that all on your own. When the time is right."

"I guess." Alice looked at the coin in her hand.

"Come on, let's take a drive. I won't keep you long. Promise. I know this is your parents' big night and don't want to keep you."

"A drive on a night like this would be nice." She curled her fingers around the coin and placed it in the toe of her shoe, hoping not to lose it.

They walked hand in hand to his convertible and got in. "Are you sure this is a good idea? Should you be driving?"

"Alice, I have lots of living to squeeze in a short amount of time. Stop worrying. I want to live life while I still have it. No more pouting."

They drove along the lake on the narrow two-lane country road.

"I've forgotten how dark these roads are without streetlights. Even with a full moon, it's hard to see through all the trees."

"Isn't it great?"

"Yes, it is, and I love it. The breeze and scent of the water is intoxicating."

Sam turned to an oldie radio station.

"I can hardly remember the girl I was back in high school. But, when I hear an old song, like what's playing now, that feeling of being young and carefree returns. It's nice reconnecting with my former teenage self and your former teenage self."

Sam pulled up to Willow Point and parked near the lake. "This is the perfect spot." He held her hand. Breathed deeply. "Alice, I need to tell you some things."

"Okay."

"You've never known your worth. I knew it then and I know it now. But back then I was too much of a coward to do anything about it, such as being a good boyfriend to you. I should have done something about my shortcomings. I should have seen you. I was just a boy. An eighteen-year-old boy who thought he knew it all."

"And now you do know it all," she teased.

"Hardly. I'm just starting. I think even in death we go on learning."

"And you found your true love, your wife, Claire."

"That I did." He smiled as he pulled out his wallet to show Alice her picture. Then he withdrew another picture and unfolded it. Two teenagers posed for the camera. The boy's hair was almost as long as the girl's, which was down to her waist. They both wore cut-off jeans.

"Us."

"I saved it all these years. We dated for a couple of years. We graduated high school. I went into the Navy. I grew up. Never saw you again. But then I found Claire. We married. It's been a good life." His hand trembled and his voice suddenly seemed weak.

What she had was photo albums filled with the past, stuck in an old trunk back at her tiny loft. It was as if she stood inside of protective glass and feelings of belonging to someone, having someone belong did not apply. Right now, she only had herself to worry about. Or not worry about. But how many women were out there, wishing for her life, as she wished for theirs?

They drove back to the party in silence. Alice slid from the car and turned toward him. "Will I see you again?" she asked, already knowing the answer.

"No." His voice cracked. He hugged her to him. "Thank you for being my friend these many years. This is my last night out. I am pleased to have spent it with you."

"Give my love to sweet Claire, and if there is anything I can do…"

He put his fingertips on her lips.

It began with a fixed stare and smile that didn't leave her face, trying to grasp, trying to understand. How odd, you can know the time and day that someone will pass, and yet, it's still a surprise. Suddenly the world seemed to drop out beneath her feet, and she dug her nails into her hands trying to keep control.

"Goodbye, my friend."

"See you later." Sam touched the end of her nose then got back into the car and drove away.

Alice lingered, watching as headlights disappeared into the darkness of trees. Death was a horrendous act to watch. One moment you are with a person you care deeply about and the very next they are swept away, as if they never were. Behind is left an empty chair, an unmade bed, shirt, shoes, a toothbrush now dry. Intangible memories. Mere vapor.

"There you are." Simon walked across the gravel driveway. "I've been looking everywhere for you."

Alice wiped her tears, hoping Simon didn't notice.

"Alice, what's wrong?"

"We can talk about it later. What's up?"

"I just couldn't find you is all."

"Hold me?"

He wrapped her into his arms, laying his head against hers. "By the way. Have you seen Megan recently?"

"It's been a while, but the last time I saw her, she was speaking to a guy by the name of Alex Godfrey."

"Who? It doesn't matter. When I couldn't find you, I thought you both had gone off somewhere to duke it out or something."

"Very funny. Let's look for her."

They searched through the clubhouse and along the lake. Finally, they had the DJ call for her over the microphone. Nothing. Then they checked the guest cottage. On the dresser was a note addressed to her and Simon. Evidently, Megan knew Alex. Charlie sent him to bring her home to him.

Alice sat on the bed and fanned herself with the letter. "I hope she went willingly."

"Let's call the police."

"She gave me Jasper. It's in the note."

"Perhaps the positive pregnancy test made her feel like going back." Fiona walked into the room.

"She's pregnant?" Simon asked.

Fiona nodded.

"Give her a few days and then let's do a welfare check," Fiona suggested, holding up her personal letter from Megan.

"I think that's a very good idea." Alice nodded.

"Tomorrow, we head home," Fiona said. "This has been so much fun."

"We will head out, but not home, not yet," Alice said.

"What are you saying, Alice?" Simon asked.

"Number three is next. Jack from Illinois."

"Jack." Simon nodded with delight.

"Who is Jack?" Fiona wanted to know.

"I refer to him as Mistake Number Three."

Chapter 28

Alice—The Affair
Illinois—*20 years earlier…*

The longing of one's heart is great, and there can be many beginnings and endings to the same relationship during a lifetime. One love unexpectedly circled back after the second set of divorce papers had been signed.

The memory of this event was bittersweet. Alice pulled back her hair into a bun, holding it in place by threading a number two pencil through it. Again she looked at the picture. Her breath caught in her chest. What was it she wanted from this picture? An accounting? An inventory of the past? No matter what it was, she was game to see him again.

He found her, or did she find him? In either case, they connected on social media. He lived in Chicago, and now she is in Texas. Alice booted up her laptop. On social network, she typed in Jack Stone and located him. Taking a deep breath, she sent a friend request, then sat for an hour waiting for him to accept it.

By morning, the obsession to see Jack grew, yet the friend request remained unanswered. Two days later, she sent him a private message online and typed, "Got the picture. Thanks. What kids we were back then. Am open to meeting. Will you be coming to the Dallas area?"

Moments later, the friend request was granted and a private message from him appeared. "Not sure about Dallas. May I be so bold as to ask your number?"

Alice was pleased with his response but decided to make him wait for her answer. It tickled her to know he wanted to see her. But, was he married? Being his 'friend' on social media, she was able to see his photos and his relationship status, which was not filled in. She was pleased to see he served in Illinois government; so, unlike the wild, untamed man he once was.

It wasn't until the next day that she sent him her cell and shop number. Within moments, he responded with his cell number along with the business office, but requested she not text, or call his cell phone evenings for that was family time with his children. Calls were rare, texts more often, but the contact on social media was rapid. They called, texted, emailed for six months—often late at night.

Then the text came: —I have never wanted anyone so much in my entire life. I must see you again.—

—Really?—

—Really. I can't stand it. I need to see you. Texting isn't enough for me. Not anymore.—

—Where are you thinking?—

—Chicago.—

—Why not Dallas?—

—I can't. My children. They live with me since the divorce.—

—Okay. Then I'll come to you.—she texted her quick answer.

"Thank you for understanding."

It occurred to her it just might be a booty call.

Quickly, she shoved away her doubts and basked in the attention he gave to her. The feelings that rose inside of her were simply erotic. Passion. How she missed this feeling.

They phoned one another daily; she at her store, and he at his office. Each conversation sounded more and more promising that their long-lost love was in the process of being reborn. And his voice. Oh, his voice. It was quiet and trailed off at the end of his sentences. Together, time became frozen, carefree, uncomplicated. It was before she made a mess of things with Simon, and marriages.

Never would she let Simon know her plans, her raw passion for Jack. Oddly, she felt guilty, as though she was cheating on her friendship with Simon. Shrugging off the nagging feeling, she realized she didn't owe Simon all the information about her life, her inner thoughts, her deep-seated longings. Some things were meant for only her. Not for Simon to tap it out on his keyboard for public consumption. And if this was a booty call, so be it. They were both consenting adults. At that time, Alice still felt good about her body. Still went to the gym.

Off to Chicago she flew, in the dress she splurged on; a lace overlay A-line pink dress with a sweetheart plunging neckline with plenty of boob to show—and due to the cold north winds, covered it over with a vintage fur coat, hoping no one would throw paint on it. Simon never knew where she went. Only that she had some important commitment. It was silly to spend the money on a plane ticket when money was tight, but it had been so long since she had felt this way—romantic and the precipice of what could be a forever love—

which made her feel giddy with the tingle of excitement—a full heart. A catch in her throat every time Jack called.

The plane landed.—I'm here!—she texted. After she located the airport's exit, she hailed a taxi and headed toward the rendezvous. A warmth in her belly grew.

And there he was, standing on Lake Shore Drive. Waiting. For. Her. The past drove him to arrive in their future. Today. This moment. Her heart stopped beating for a breath as they waved. Rosy cheeks from the sharp cold, she leaped from the cab and hurried toward the predesignated corner of the meeting. A sharp wind snapped the breath from her lungs. And then here he came, crossing four lanes of highly busy traffic, on foot. Not a smart move, but an impressive one. His eyes were on her, not on the cars that beeped at him to get out of their way.

It seemed like an instant and he was right there in front of her. He rocked on his feet, smiling, looking down at her as though considering her for the very first time. She had forgotten how tall he was. They laughed nervously at the same time.

"Hey, stranger." With a flourish, he unwrapped the scarf from around his neck and used it to pull her toward him before tugging her into him with his big bear arms.

Alice felt herself grin ear to ear looking into his face. Same blue eyes. Dark brown hair that curled at the nap of his neck. Disarming smile. Her arms hung at her side—not quite sure what to do with them. Slowly she inserted them into her coat pockets. She had prepared a speech for him, but it floated off into the snowy sky. He wrapped her up in his arms and kissed her long and hard and with such great passion that she no longer had a thought of anything or anyone but this. All thoughts of the world around them faded away. Jack took her hand and led her through the streets as though she had no will of her own. A warm sensation whirred in her belly. A hypnotic sense of safety and calm took over.

At the five-star hotel, he paid cash for their room. The ride up in the elevator was a bit awkward. Silence. She watched the numbers above the door light up, trying to make small talk. Jack unlocked the door to their hotel room. Alice walked directly to the windows, as though it was a movie scene, and looked out at Lake Michigan, frozen over by winter. He walked up behind her and pulled her hair to the side to kiss her neck. "Let's get undressed," he whispered. Feeling his breath on her throat gave her chills.

She quietly nodded wondering why she was unable to speak; so willing to do whatever he asked of her. "Take off your clothes." She did.

"Leave your jewelry on the bedside table." She did.

"Get into bed." She did.

He crawled toward her. Deep, hungry kisses caressed her breasts, neck and finally her mouth, his tongue shoving itself around, exploring her teeth, her tongue. He climbed on top as she spread her legs wide. He jabbed himself into her and she gave a small scream.

"Did I hurt you?" he asked apologetically.

"Go deeper."

He did.

"Harder."

He did.

"Faster."

He did.

Hours later, they both were totally exhausted from a day of being in bed together. She made a mental note to get a gym membership to better keep up with him the next time they were together.

With only a few hours until departure, Jack grew oddly silent. Remote. If she allowed it, she'd also surrender to depression because their day was nearly done. Alice dressed in the bathroom and then sat on the end of the bed, waiting, hoping, for reassurance there would be a next time. After all, they were adults. Long ago, she was beautifully deflowered by Simon Davenport. Her heart was ready to move along to the next chapter with Jack. For now, she wouldn't tell Simon. Never would know about today. It was much too precious to share.

No cab this time. It was his idea to drive her to the airport. She made small talk. He watched the traffic. Alice imagined him as devastated as she that the day had drawn to a close. Jack pulled to the curb and stopped the car, leaving the engine running. He looked at her from the corner of his eye and suddenly bolted from the car. She quickly exited, trying to emerge like Grace Kelley, wanting to make a lasting impression. A gracious, ladylike impression. Stone-faced, Jack pulled her out of his car with one hand.

"I'm not good at goodbyes." She tearfully reached for him.

"Then let's make this quick." He artfully dodged her hug and placed his hand under her elbow to hurry her toward the airport doors where he gave her a small shove, got back into his car and peeled off.

After catching her breath while still standing at the window doors, Alice walked toward the gate, stopping to purchase a few boxes of Fannie May Candies, something that couldn't be found in the South. On the plane, she replayed the afternoon. Though their parting wasn't picture perfect, everything else was, so she felt good about their day together. After all, the airport was a busy spot. Parking was at a premium. Yet, his sudden coolness toward her late in the day seemed odd, out of place, but whatever caused it would be cleared by tomorrow—or tonight, when they chatted on the phone. Or texted.

Once the wheels had touched the tarmac, she grabbed her carry-on and walked to her car in the same spot she had left it only twelve hours earlier. As she headed north up I-35, she decided first to swing by the antique store. It had only been one day, not even a twenty-four-hour day, but she needed to make sure that in her absence nothing had changed. She looked at her cell, hoping for, expecting some endearing message from Jack. Conjuring up the lovely things, he would say to her. Nothing.

Nearly nine o'clock, her assistant Stella was just locking up.

"Oh, Alice. I didn't expect you until tomorrow. Want me to stay longer?"

"No, go on home. There are a few things I need to do before heading home." An unnatural feeling of nerves settled in the pit of her stomach. "By the way, have there been any calls for me this evening?"

"No, none." Stella smiled. "Did you have fun on your buying trip in Chicago?"

"Buying trip?" Alice asked, confused.

Stella held up a brochure about a huge auction taking place along Chicago's Lakeshore drive that day.

"Oh." Alice didn't know anything about it. "Where did that come from?"

"I found it here in the shop. I thought it was yours. You were going to Chicago, so I just kind of put it all together."

"Oh. I see. No, didn't find anything interesting for the shop." The last thing on her mind was a Chicago auction. She'd never recoup her monies with shipping costs even if she found something scrumptious unless it could fit in a box. Alice looked around as though something might be missing.

Stella grabbed her jacket and headed to the street.

Alice stood over the phone, wanting to call Jack. The expected bevy of calls from Illinois never materialized. Not by cell or landline. What was wrong? Could he have gotten into a car wreck? Were his children demanding his usual attention? Did he fall asleep after such a passionate day? It was tempting to text him if only to say she arrived home safely. Just then the old shop bell over the door tingled.

A beautiful young Hispanic woman entered wearing thigh-high boots over tight jeans and a shawl over a sweater. "Are you closing? I know it's late. I saw a few things here earlier today and should have picked them up then, but had to go home and measure, then I got busy."

"No problem. Come on in. What can I do for you?"

"Are you the owner? I thought we could discuss the price if I buy several items."

"Of course, I love to bundle. I'm Alice, by the way." She held out her hand.

"I'm Talia Arroyo. Nice to meet you." They shook hands.

"By the way, I love your kidney-shaped sofa toward the back." Talia walked across the floor and ran her fingers along the fabric.

"You have great taste. It's a French-carved mahogany sofa. The cushions are down."

"Amazing."

"Yes, it is. Original fabric. Do you have children?"

"Not yet. But they won't be allowed to sit there when I do." She laughed.

"Tell me, what is your home like? The style?" Alice asked.

"Cottage."

Alice felt stunned. "Cottage? It's none of my business, but why would you mix the house with the wrong pieces that will fight? Let me show you something else. Follow me." Alice walked to the back room. "Look, a mission Stickley couch."

"It's gorgeous. And should fit beautifully in my home."

"It's expensive, but I will price it just for you."

"You are an angel," Talia gushed.

After striking a deal and scheduling a delivery date with Talia, Alice hurried home. It unexpectedly felt good to be here. So much had happened in the last day and it made her feel she had changed, while everything else remained quite the same.

Again, she checked her cell in case there was a text or call she had missed. Nope. Neither. She checked the volume. It was all the way up. As soon as Alice set the cell on her dresser and disrobed, her cell beeped, causing her heart to race.

"Hello!" she answered, not looking at the Caller I.D.

"Did you have a good day?"

"Simon." Her heart dropped.

"Just called to make sure you got home safely."

"I am home. I am safe."

"Good."

"Thanks for calling, Simon. And for checking on me."

"That's my job. Goodnight."

After a shower, she lay in bed thinking about what a good guy Simon was. How she could always count on him. She realized men and women approached things so differently. That was it. Here she was wide awake with worry, and he was most likely asleep with a big smile on his face.

****

Sunshine touched every part of her body that wound around her white sheets. She blinked eyes open wide. It was barely eight and the sun was full in the sky illuminating the street below. College kids' voices carried up to her open window as cars rumbled past.

Her first thought was of him and their day spent in a Chicago hotel bed—wasn't that just yesterday? By midnight she had dropped into a dead man's sleep and didn't remember the phone ringing. Had she missed Jack's call? With a jolt, she sat upright and reached for her cell. No call. No text. She frowned. She panicked. What was wrong?

Befuddled about his silence, she hurried to the bathroom where she showered and dressed, at the same time, coming up with a dozen lame excuses why he hadn't contacted her. Of course, there was his thriving business and teenage kids he had ignored for a day that needed catching up on. By tonight there'd be a flurry of calls and texts. Maybe flowers too. She was sure of it. In the meantime, she needed to be confident and not so needy.

The hours slowly, painfully ticked by without a word until two days had passed. By now she was frantic, wildly texting him, begging for a reply while peppering him with questions: was he okay? Was his phone dead? Did one of his kids get sick? Had she disappointed him?

His answer came, finally. By. Way. Of. Text. Reading it, created a hole in her heart too big to be patched. She sank to her knees.

She held up her cell and reread.

—Alice, I lied. I'm married. I am riddled with guilt. Our affair is over.—

Chapter 29

Present Day—Chicago
Simon
Midnight

—Are you asleep?—
—Dozing.—
—Want to talk?—
—Not really.—
—Come to me.—
—Now?—
—Yes.—

He closed the text.

He watched as the door opened and she stepped into the darkened room.

"Hello?"

"Lock the door."

She did.

"Don't turn on the light."

"I won't."

He opened the covers to her. As she walked toward him in bed, she laughed. "What do you have on?"

"Pajamas."

"They're striped." She laughed.

He patted the place next to him.

"Should I take off my clothes? At least my slacks?"

"Up to you."

She slid in next to him, fully clothed. He covered her and wrapped his arms around her. She faced away from him. He felt the warmth of her body nestling into him. Spooning like a couple.

"What's this all about?" she asked.

"Tell me about Jack," Simon asked. He turned on the tape recorder on the nightstand. There was something special about him, he sensed it. How special was he and why? Was there still a connection between them? What would he do if there were? Jealousy and fear nagged.

"Are you kidding me?" She jumped up. "You called me to come to tell you another story? A bedtime story?"

He patted the bed again. "Pillow talk time."

She complied and lay facing him, squeezing a pillow between them as he restarted the recorder.

"Why is Jack Stone important to you?"

"Suffice it to say, Jack taught me a lesson." She moved about to get comfortable.

"Which was?"

"Let's just say, this one is a journey of closure." She now stared at the ceiling.

"Another closure?" Simon wanted to hear more.

"I thought this is what the trip is all about, right? Opening old doors to see what I left." Alice explained their relationship as children and then as teens. She finally told him about his contact via mail with her ten years earlier and flying to Chicago to see him.

"Why do I feel you're leaving something out?"

She hesitated.

"Alice." Simon didn't like she was holding back.

"It's my business."

She turned her head to avoid his gaze.

"I thought we were past all that personal business crap. Alice, we are on an assignment here. I need you to be open. If it's something we don't need in the book, then I won't use it. Let's discuss it first."

"Oh, okay." She took in a gulp of air before continuing. "It involves a hotel room."

"Okay." He wasn't so sure he liked hearing about her sexual exploits though they were few and far between. He noticed her sudden silence. "It involved a hotel room. Go on."

"And a lie. I don't want to get him into trouble with—anyone. And I refuse to humiliate myself in the process." She sighed deeply.

"I understand. He's a jerk. I hate guys like him." Simon was speaking more about himself than this Jack person she never mentioned. The pain in her eyes sliced him. The betrayal she suffered because of him made him wince. He knew he was just one of the guys who hurt her.

"Yeah, you and me both hate guys like him. There are too many of them out in the world." She managed a small smile. "It took me a year to get over him. I never hurt that badly, not even with my divorces. It hurt to even breathe for a while. It was silly because I allowed myself to believe that this was the real thing. On the bright side, I learned a valuable lesson."

"Tell me." His heart ached for her.

"Relationships are a journey. They take time. If you want a shallow relationship, or to be used, then jump right into bed. Yes, and it doesn't escape me that we are together in bed right now."

"I'm guilty of that—with you."

"Oh, Simon, please, let's not go there. I didn't know anything back then—neither did you. We've become best friends over the years." She reached across the space between them and touched his hand. "Let that one go. I have."

"You are too generous."

"This is my advice that I want included in the book. If you desire someone to withstand the test of time, be patient and wait. Waiting takes you to a deeper level of knowing someone that cannot be known with sex stuff going on."

"I like the advice and would like to use it. I want to use the story as well."

Nervously she jiggled her foot."We can change Jack's name and location."

"I already did that."

"What are you saying?"

"The name and location aren't important. The event is. Whatever happens today is important."

"Alice, do you think you're the only one this has happened to? He's the schmuck here. Not you."

"I walked into the situation with my eyes wide open. Heart before reason."

"Because you felt he was genuine—and for some reason he wasn't. Your heart was in the right place."

"But my body wasn't. It was in a hotel room with a married man."

"Stop."

"Stop what?"

"With me, you shouldn't feel ashamed or embarrassed." He took her hand. "A hint of guilt still hangs over you like a dark cloud, even after all these years. Let it go."

"Decisions shape our destiny. I'd like a do-over and recast myself. I'm easy to move on from—to dismiss. Even invisible at times, like something that slips behind a dresser and is forgotten." Alice's tears threatened, but she retracted them by pressing her eyelids. "There are periods in my life that I wanted to slip behind a dresser and disappear into a crack in the floor."

"Alice, I understand. It's normal." If his love was brave enough, he would have crossed the emotional distance between them and shown his love for her all night long. But in her fragile state of mind, he knew she wasn't ready—not yet. He wanted her to come to him fully with no regrets. "Normal is being loved. Guilt will stop you from living—from taking chances."

"Guilt? I am riddled with it." She stared at him and looked from him to the door. "It's late. I should go."

Simon didn't want to let her go. He wanted to wrap his arms around her and protect her from what might happen when she saw Jack in the morning. It made him wonder if she'd fall for him once again. And then what? So many questions he could tell she wasn't ready to answer.

"By the way, I'm not telling Jack about you, or this project. So, I am going in solo on this one." She carefully got up from the bed, trying her best not to reveal her hip pain that had somehow gotten worse since the trip started. She still wanted to appear young and vivacious to Simon although, at this moment, she felt more middle-aged and worn out. As she started toward the door she found herself limping.

"Are you hurting?"

"No, just aging." She looked back at him, then

turned the doorknob to leave.

"Not the usual podcast banter, then?" He knew this could be disastrous especially if she repeated her last mistake with him—and then wondered if he was still married, or even single by now. It suddenly occurred to him that if he were single again, Alice might cave. After all, it seemed as though she still carried lost desire.

"No, I'll handle this on my own. We won't use his real name in the book. And we can use a stand-in for the picture later."

"Alice."

She turned toward him again slowly.

"Stay with me tonight—please." Now he was the one begging. "Just sleep with me. Nothing more. Promise."

She didn't respond.

He couldn't take his eyes from her—not even to blink. "I just want to hold you. Look, we can lay on top of the blankets with just a throw over us. I want to be with you tonight. Whatever comes tomorrow, I want to sleep with you tonight. And I do mean sleep. I won't take advantage, not when you feel so vulnerable." He felt he had seen into her soul and wanted to hold onto it.

She smiled at him and walked out.

Chapter 30

Jack
Chicago—The Next Day

Jack Stone stood on Lakeshore Drive. The hotel where they once spent a lovely day together. He patted his stomach and tried sucking it in. With thirty-five added pounds, he couldn't help but feel self-conscious to see her again. Even so, he still couldn't resist seeing her, being with her. He needed a repeat of that passion.

After admitting he was married, he was fully aware he was the villain in their story. It never surprised him she severed the relationship. It was for the best. From time to time, he allowed himself to replay that erotic day in his mind, not completely ready to release Alice from his thoughts. He remembered how animated she acted. Filled with joy. Before parting ways, he had taken a long, hot shower to wipe her perfume and organic scent away.

As he emerged from the shower, he caught his reflection in the large bathroom mirror. His ego and smile dropped. There he was, an old gray guy with a pouched belly.

After dropping her at the airport, Jack drove home, anxious to see his wife, afraid she'd sense his unfaithfulness. This dalliance couldn't be discovered. At all costs, he had to protect his family.

Yet, it was hard letting go of Alice. No matter how many calls and emails he made to her afterward telling her he was married, that he needed to see her again and again, she never responded. Years later, while on social media, he sent her a friend request; embarrassed to do so and almost humiliated. A month later, she accepted it. Their talk was anything but sexual. But her coming to Chicago was going to be sexual. Very sexual. He couldn't wait.

After her recent open invitation to meet, after so long, he figured she might still be thinking about that day together again too. He would do anything for a reenactment and pocketed a bottle of Viagra just in case. The room was booked. Same floor. Same room. He was ready. No bed cover would be left unturned by the time they were finished with one another.

And there she was. Hurrying from a cab toward him. The dress was blue. Her waist wasn't belted, her breasts were tucked into the top. Alice was the embodiment of fashion. He wanted her badly. Jack hadn't felt like this since their last meeting.

Just as he leaned to kiss her, she turned her head. He tried to take her hand. She withdrew. They started down the street. She took his arm but for only a moment.

"What?" There was something a bit off. He had hurt her. Disappointed her. What could he do to win her over? There were off-putting signals coming his way, such as refusing to go directly to their room for one. She was hungry and needed to be fed, she said with a toss of the head. He tried to whisper in her ear, but she pulled away with a soft giggle.

If she needed to do this to prove something to him,

he'd do it. There was a small eatery he took her to where they sat by a window. Her eyes were bright, and her cheeks blushed as she spoke. It mesmerized him to watch how she held her fork and the way she drank from the edge of the water glass, leaving a trace of lipstick behind. Those lips belonged on his skin—to cover his body. He yearned for her familiar flesh, for his bone against her. Inside of her.

"I'm really looking forward to being with you again." He spoke softly. Women liked that.

"I'm looking forward to this afternoon, as well." She looked at him from the top of her eyes. Her foot slid across the floor to top the toe of his shoe.

Alice's smile gave him warm chills. He knew then there would be no need for artificial stimulation.

The day fluttered by with conversation which Jack found perplexing. He was anxious to get to the room, take her clothes off, and his. Just the thought of their clothes lying across the floor was unbearable. By late afternoon, after lunch, a gallery showing, and shopping where he bought her a diamond necklace, they finally approached the hotel's lobby where he again paid cash for the room. Just like the last time, twenty years earlier.

He took her by the elbow and steered her toward the elevator. His breaths became faster and shallower.

"Be patient." She took a step back and pressed her finger to his lips. "I am as anxious as you. But first things first. I have something special planned. Go on up without me. I need to order something from the dining room." She nodded toward a cart of champagne with chocolate-covered strawberries. Slowly walking down the hallway, he heard her ordering it to be delivered to their room, pronto.

When he reached the floor, he slipped the key into the lock and opened the door to the suite. Immediately he headed to the bathroom where he removed his clothes and took a full dose of Viagra—just in case there was last moment failure to launch. He sucked in his gut and turned sideways looking at himself in the mirror. Maybe he would wait here until she came to the room. No, he didn't want to pop out of the bathroom, bad form. There, on the back of the bathroom door, was a hotel robe which he slipped on just as he heard the door to the suite open. A cart rattled in.

"Oh, thank you so very much," he heard her say.

When the door shut, he walked out. There she was. Curtains wide open, standing by the windows, looking out on Lake Michigan. But instead of the cold of winter, it was the warmth of summer. Alice had changed her hair a bit—pinned to the top of her head. Ah, his girl knew he loved removing the pins one by one. Such a turn-on. And she wore a long see-through negligee.

"Oh my, but I have waited so long for this. I cannot stand it a moment longer." Just then he noticed the box that held the necklace he had bought for her was on the cart, opened.

He looked back at the window.

"I hope you're wearing my necklace."

"Necklace? What necklace?" She turned around.

Jack's eyes grew wide in horror and outermost surprise.

It wasn't Alice.

It was Beth.

"What a nice surprise, Jack. I got the call from the

hotel manager this morning and here I am."

"Welcome to Chicago." Dave's face paled and his knees buckled, but then recovered quickly to greet his wife.

Chapter 31

"It was hard keeping a poker face."
"But you pulled it off."
Alice sat with Simon under a hot city sky at dusk along Lake Michigan. They found a bench over the water on Navy Pier and sat. Simon already had too much to drink due to the unfolding events of the day, waiting for Alice, and laid down with his head in her lap, arms crossed over his midriff. They were together in the middle of the busy dock. Alice was pierced with joy and wild imagination.

"I am a girl who likes to be remembered. This is a day he will never forget."

"When did you come up with the idea of calling his wife for a rendezvous?"

"It's been a while in the making." She gently ran her fingers through his hair. Simon grabbed her hand and kissed the back of it before holding it to his face. "This morning, right before I met Jack, I called his wife, pretending to be the hotel manager. I said, as a surprise, her husband had booked the hotel room for the weekend. To arrive by four."

"That was powerful, Alice." Simon laughed. "I sure wish I could have seen his face when he saw his wife instead of you."

"Me too, but if I imagine it correctly, I think he probably looked something like this." Alice's jaw slacked and she made her eyes large.

They burst out laughing.

"And how do you feel now?"

"I feel wonderful!" Alice clapped. "A bit vindicated and forgiven. Free."

"Forgiven?"

"I have forgiven myself." It was shocking to learn that the man in front of her knew about her self-blame.

"Will you keep him as a friend on social media?"

"I don't think that would be productive—no. I've already blocked him." She carefully measured her words before starting again. "And thank you for last night."

"What about last night?"

"For being a friend and a gentleman."

"Men hate being referred to as 'friend'." He shuttered.

"What are we then, if not friends?"

"More than a friend." He reached for her and kissed the back of her hand.

There was a pause in the conversation as Alice noticed a tall, blonde, well-muscled man ogling her. He gave a half wave and began to walk toward them.

"Oh, my goodness. It's you," the gorgeous man called to her.

"Excuse me? Do I know you?"

"Alice?"

"Yes."

"Well, you used to know me."

"Oh dear." She didn't know if it was because she was tired after such a long day, but lately, she had started forgetting things, like people's faces and names. Last month she had forgotten one of her best customer's names. How could she forget her?

Simon sat up with a slight grimace on his face.

"Sorry, I'm Lance Beck." The man held out his hand but she still didn't move. He looked at his empty hand before inserting it into his pocket. "I can tell by your expression you don't remember me."

"I am so sorry."

"I can't blame you. There must be so many men winking and poking you."

"Excuse me." Simon stood to his feet, striking a poise to defend.

"Oh, okay. I can see I am misunderstood. It's terminology that is used on dating sites."

"Now I remember you. Lance, yes. You are a biga-biga—"

"Biologist."

"Sorry, I meant biologist. You just caught me off guard."

"That's right, and you didn't want to get together because you lived in Texas while I live in Illinois. I believe the term you used was 'geographically undesirable'."

"Ah, you are right. I am so sorry."

"And here you are anyway, in Chicago." He looked around at the buildings as though he needed to verify to her where she was.

"Just an impromptu business visit." Remembering Simon, she added, "This is my friend, ohm, boss, Simon. Simon, this is Lance."

Simon held out his hand.

Lance responded.

"Well, I think I will get going. It'll give you two a chance to chat without the winks and pokes." Simon walked several yards down the pier and held onto the railing, staring down at the water. Alice noted he was keeping a watch on them which gave her a tingle of happiness.

Lance sat beside Alice. She noted he was more handsome than his pictures, which was unusual. She was used to men posting photographs that were ten years younger than they truly are. One man even said he was an avid athlete and named the sports he participated in, but when they met, he could hardly walk.

"A biologist." She shifted in the opposite direction a little. "Are you a teacher?"

"I work at the University of Chicago—in research."

"Oh. I suppose you already told me this?" She ran her tongue over her palate in an attempt to find moisture since her mouth suddenly went dry.

Lance nodded. "You are much prettier in person."

"Thanks. And you are—taller than I imagined."

"Is there something going on between you and your boss?" He cast his eyes toward Simon.

"Oh, no, no." Alice insisted, smiling as though he had said something funny.

"Since you're here, in Chicago, how about dinner?"

"Oh, I don't know. I'm here with friends and already promised we would do something together."

"Why don't you invite them along too? Unless one is your boyfriend."

"No. No. They are both friends."

"Let's go for drinks?"

Alice looked over her shoulder at Simon who

quickly turned his head away, trying to seem he wasn't watching. "Lance, any other time and I would've accepted, but not today."

The man slowly rose to his feet. "I understand." He turned to go but then stopped. "Does your boss know you are in love with him?"

"In love with him?" Her throat got drier. "That's absurd. We're just good friends."

Lance glanced down the pier toward Simon and caught his eye. "He loves you too."

"I-I…" What was that fluttering in the pit of her stomach anyway?

"Take care of yourself." He squeezed her hand before heading toward Wabash Avenue.

Out of the blue, Lance's words made Alice rethink Simon's and her relationship. Did he see something she was blind to? Of course, she had always hoped for something more from the man than a platonic relationship but she also accepted it as a dream, a prayer, a wish, an impossibility. Staring down the pier at Simon, she realized he did act in a romantic sort of manner from time to time, but then he'd vanish for weeks without a word, or say something contrary to how she thought he might be feeling—as though he needed her more substantially—friendship—and therefore never lose one another. Friendship was a slippery slope because it could be disguised as romance. Was Alice merely sleepwalking through life wishing he loved her, and instead of being embraced by his arms, she bumped into walls?

That night at dinner, Alice felt distracted as she sorted through her twisted emotions, watching Simon's every move and analyzing his words as though there was a vocabulary exam on their meaning in the morning. Simon was a friend who occasionally crossed the line into romance, but just as quickly kept himself in check, reordering himself as a trusted confidante; partner in crime. Not only did Lance seem to spot something between them, but Talia had as well. Sometimes standing afar can see more clearly than someone standing too close.

"By the way, Alice, I like your dress. Sexy," Simon said before taking a long sip of iced water. As the words left his mouth, they floated across the table and made her lightheaded. Making her smile. Making her heart fill with joy. Alice couldn't help but glance at Fiona, wondering about her reaction, but she seemed too consumed ordering dinner than to react.

Amazing how optimistic she suddenly felt with waves of hope washing over her. He called her 'sexy' it was a sign. She knew it. Everything was going to be okay.

Then Simon started a conversation with Fiona. Did he say sweet things to her too? Or just to her? And today who was the recipient of his sweetest, most flattering words? And as they sat here, who did Simon speak to the most? Who held his attention the most between the two—three of them if Megan was included? Was there still hope for her? Alice knocked down her third glass of wine.

"Isn't that your fourth glass?" Simon asked.

"Third. But the fourth is on its way soon. Waiter?" She held up her glass. "Why aren't you drinking, Simon?"

"I never drink when I'm on a story."

"Ah, the story," she said as the waiter refilled her

glass.

"Of all the times we've had dinner together, you never even finish one glass of wine. I've never seen you drink like this," Simon said with a look of concern.

"Me either. I've never seen me drink like this. It's so relaxing. I'm going to do it more."

Simon turned on his cell recorder. "Ladies, what advice would you give to other women about forming relationships?"

"Too bad my mother isn't here. She is so good at this advice giving out stuff. It could have been very helpful to me as a teenager if I only had paid attention to it. Maybe that's where it all went wrong. But Mother had her rules and she lived by them. I have no rules. Ask Zeba. I wasn't a bad example. I wasn't a good example. I was just an example."

"And thank you for that," Simon cut in. "Who wants to go first?"

"I will," Alice quickly piped up again feeling quite tipsy. "Build a strong friendship first. If you cannot build a strong friendship, then you will never be able to maintain a solid relationship. And no sex. Not for months and months and more months. Not even if he begs you for it."

"I think you've had plenty to drink, Alice." Simon took the glass from her hand.

"Profound, Alice."

"Thanks, Fiona. If I only had known that and applied it when I was younger. It would have saved a lot of heartache. Where's the waiter? I need more wine."

"Okay, my turn." Fiona cleared her throat. "Take time to get to know yourself. Then you will know the right person when he arrives on the scene and quickly marry him. That's what I did. I got found true love and married him. But he died. And now I am adrift."

"Where's the waiter? I need more wine," Alice repeated.

There were a few minutes of silence.

"I wish I could get Megan's advice on men."

"Advice on men? I'd love to give mine." The flamboyant waiter delivered a fresh glass of wine to Alice and set three bowls of soup on the table.

"We are all listening." Simon made sure the tape recorder was still running.

"Don't settle for less than what you know you need."

"We do that too often, don't we?" Alice now spoon-sipped her crab soup, dribbling some on herself. "Oh, this is wonderful. Anyone want a taste?"

"Would you all excuse me? I have other tables."

"Yes. And thank you for your input."

"I suddenly feel so tired."

In the hotel room, Alice plopped down in the middle of her bed. She rolled over and clasped her hands behind her head in thought as Jasper ate the leftover dinner.

Where was Megan tonight? Was she happy? Was she resting in Charlie's arms as a happy couple, or was he berating her for leaving? If a dog wasn't safe around him, surely Megan and a baby wouldn't be either. How Alice wished she had offered her a haven in Denton.

Chapter 32

Alice
The next day…

"I feel lobotomized." Alice inched toward the SUV wearing large sunglasses and holding a water bottle in one hand and a box of saltines in the other.

"Not feeling so well today, I see." Simon grinned.

"Hangover," she muttered as her stomach lurched, trying not to vomit again, and hopeful no one could smell it in her hair. "I'm never drinking again. Not a drop."

"Next stop New Orleans," Fiona announced.

"Stop screaming, will you?" Alice rubbed her forehead.

"I think there will be a night spent in a hotel somewhere between here and there."

"Thank goodness," Alice whispered.

For what seemed like hours, traffic slowed for rush hour with Simon muttering obscenities at the drivers. There was little to look at but the back end of a black minivan and the rusted undercarriage of a green truck. When they stopped for dinner, Simon bought her an ice pack to hold on her face and several water bottles. She felt somewhat better but now was dizzy with hunger.

Back on the road, Alice shut her eyes. For the next hour, he commented on the path of the setting sun, the

SUV's air conditioner, a driver in the next car who was talking on their cell, plus counted all the state police cars without missing a beat. It seemed he had nothing better to do than deliver observances.

"Fiona, you looked pretty today."

Her hair ran in lazy waves down her back to her shoulder blades. "Thank you. I took extra long in the bathroom this morning."

"You didn't eat much for lunch, Alice," Simon said.

A cell buzzed. "Zeba, is this really you?"

"I guess you've heard what a mess I've made of things."

"Never mind that. Are you all right?"

"I've gone away for a little while."

"Where to? Tell me. I'll come to you."

"Mother, I don't want you to come. I told you that I've made a mess of things and I need to be alone for a while. I'm only calling to let you know that I'm all right."

"I'm glad you called." Alice rubbed her forehead in hopes it would quell her building headache. "Don't worry about anything. I should be home in a few days and take care of everything."

"But the shop and Thalia's baby room…You were right all along about me."

"I am sure nothing has been done that cannot be fixed. And as for you, you are smart and talented. When you heal, come home. I need your help in my shop. I want you to be my apprentice to someday take over."

"Really, Mom?"

"Yes. And Zeba. I love you."

"Love you too, Mom. I'll contact you again when I

am feeling better."

"Take care of yourself, honey." The call ended.

Now the tears came. "That was Zeba."

"We heard."

"Is there nothing you aren't commenting on today, Simon?"

"You're upset."

Fiona burst out laughing. "Oh, Alice, you sure do crack me up."

"What's the latest on hers and Martin's break up?" Simon asked.

"How should I know; I'm only her mother. She isn't telling me anything. But she tells my mother, of all people."

Simon reached for her hand. "You're a good mom. And Zeba will figure things out for herself. Just try to be patient. Hey, I have an idea."

"Let's hear it." Fiona clapped. "I'm a fan of ideas."

"I know I said we'd stop for the night, but I don't feel tired at all. How about you girls get more comfortable and I'll drive all night. I have an idea for a picture I want to take in New Orleans but I need the morning light. If we stop, I'll miss it."

"It's fine with me. How about you, Alice?"

"Let's drive."

Chapter 33

Alice and Simon
Saying Goodbye
Mid-July

Fiona stood at the curb waving. Her bright pink luggage was beside her on the pavement.

"Come visit, Fiona," Alice called out the window. "Make it soon."

"I will," Fiona answered back. "Promise. I am so glad you and I are besties now. I just knew it would happen."

"Ya know, I'm going to miss that girl." Alice turned about as they headed home.

"Me too. Now, that wasn't too bad with Fiona, was it?"

"Not at all. She grew on me. A sincerely nice person. However, I do worry about Megan. I only wanted to protect her."

"It's her choice."

"I realize that. And now she's pregnant." Alice sighed. "I can't believe she just left without a word. It might have helped if I'd been nicer to her, so in a way, I feel I'm part of the reason she decided to leave."

"You don't know that for sure. Let yourself off the hook. Onward toward Texas. I'd say that the entire trip went pretty darn well. Lots of surprises along the way."

He gave a sideways glance.

"There sure were, and I wouldn't have changed a thing. I'm glad you talked me into it."

"You are welcome. By the way, how are things at the shop? Have you heard anything?"

"Yes, I have. In fact, I've been in contact with Stella every few days, I just didn't want to spoil our trip with bulletins." Alice stared out at the passing trees.

"That doesn't sound good."

"Stella said Martin's cooking classes brought in lots of customers the first few weeks. But since the breakup, that is now defunct. I wonder where my antiques were moved. I will find them and put them back together. In the meantime, I'm coming up with new ideas to generate more revenue."

"Atta girl. What have you planned?"

"Why not do something interesting with the two places? I thought of creating rooms within each shop as if it were a house. Each room would be a theme keeping in with a particular time period. There'll be furnished bedrooms, dining room, kitchen, living room, and so forth. Primitives would be in one section of the shop, then the Victorian era, art deco, mid-century modern, and so forth."

"Sounds like a whole lot of work. Your shop isn't that big."

"Stella mentioned the shop next door is for rent."

"And the dream of your vintage house moves off into the sunset?"

"We shall see." Alice crossed her arms. "I'll be busy that is for sure. It might be exactly what I need."

"I'm still giving you the entire check from the publisher plus fifty percent of sales."

"Whoa, look at you, Mister Money Pants, and the book isn't even in existence. I just might have something up my sleeve as well."

Simon squeezed her hand. "Let's talk about it later and meanwhile enjoy the drive. There's time to sort it all out."

Hours later they arrived. First stop, the loft. Simon dragged Alice's suitcases up the steps as she searched through cabinets. "I need a drink." Finding an unopened bottle of wine, she held it up.

"It's late."

"No, don't you dare leave. You are drinking with me." Alice carried the bottle and two plastic tumblers to the coffee table. She sat, kicked off her shoes, and put her feet under her.

Simon laughed and took a seat next to her. He held up his glass and gave a toast. "To us. We did it."

"To us and the book."

"And to your new house. And new ventures."

"To my new house and new ventures," she repeated. "I am so excited. I can see it now; a front porch with gables. The kitchen sink overlooking the backyard. Original hardwood floors throughout the place."As she sipped her wine, she thought about what else she wanted in her vintage home and to make sure things went smoothly from here on. She wanted to be debt-free but worry-free as well. With Simon at her side and royalties, she just may have it all.

As for what awaited her at the shop, she was too tired to make a to-do list. Besides, the wine made her woozy after the long drive. The feeling was lovely. She'd enjoy its effects. Maybe she'd get lucky with Simon finally.

The sight of him in her tiny living room, sitting on the pullout couch, required her immediate attention. His body with a small pouch of a tummy leaning out over the band of his blue jeans, his large hands that spend hours and hours holding onto the steering wheel. His curly hair. His thin lips and how they moved when he shaped his words. Simon was delicious in every way. She drank another tumbler of wine, followed by another.

Simon finished his single glass and then rubbed his hands together as though he were cold.

"To our special kind of friendship. May it last for another decade or two. Maybe even three if we both live that long." She held her glass and then drank down her fourth glass. "I do believe I have emptied the bottle. Should we go out for more?"

"I'm fine, and you have had enough, my dear."

"My part of my book is completed." Alice sighed in relief.

"You mean your part of my book is completed."

"Okay."

"Now the harder work for me is just beginning. Pictures and story," Simon continued.

Alice sat back filled with a warmth growing over her body and her mind numbed. "I think it's time to concentrate on us."She threw her arms up and then settled them into her lap as she looked in his direction.

Simon answered by placing his arm around her. Her desire grew as he kissed her neck, her cheeks, her lips. She responded in kind, placing her arms around him. "Three decades have passed since our tete-a-tete. I'm ready for another."

He drew her against him, pulling out the shirt from

the back of her jeans, running his hands down to her buttocks where he squeezed them firmly. A quick orgasm made her cry out as Simon fingered her.

They jumped off the couch and pulled it out, back into a bed. She laid on her back, parting her legs after flinging her blouse and bra across the room. Simon stood over her. His gaze roamed over her entire body, then pulled his pants off and flung them over his head.

On top of her, his hardness against her groin and the wine in her belly made her wet with desire.

"Take off your damn briefs."

"Slow down just a bit. I am older."

Simon fingered her again then sucked her juice from his fingers.

"We need to make up for lost time." He kissed her ear.

"I have loved you for so long. Forever it seems." She paused for a moment to ask, "Lost time? Exactly how does one do that? Make up for lost time—how does one do that?" She pulled back to look at him. His face was so adorable that she raked his hair back with her hand.

"By making the most of what we have right now." Simon lifted himself slightly off her to rub his hand between her legs. His voice was tender. "Now, sshhh."

"And what would that look like, exactly?"

"You are making this really hard on me." He looked at his waning crotch.

"Things go wrong in life. Details are important. I need something to hold onto."

"Hold onto me." He took her hand and placed it between his legs. "And I have a confession."

"Confession? Sounds intriguing." She pumped his

cock.

Simon turned on his side and looked pensively at Alice as he stopped the movement of her hand on him."I was there."

"Huh? Where?" Alice withdrew her hand.

"On your wedding day. The day you married Thomas."

"Simon, you couldn't have been there. I didn't see you." Chills pricked her arm as she propped herself on her elbows. "I looked for you."

"When your wedding invitation arrived, I was furious. And then I realized I was furious because I didn't want anyone to have you except for me. After I got there, I had second thoughts about ruining your day. I figured you had to be in love with Thomas. After all, it was your wedding day. You were marrying the guy." He circled her face with his fingers.

"I had no idea."She kissed his fingertips.

And suddenly, the years seemed to melt away. She imagined seeing herself as a young bride at the altar. Simon appeared. Not as a guest but as the groom. How long would they have been married if things worked out? Children? Grandparents?

"A day before the wedding, I decided to take action. I called your house, your mother's house, and asked to speak to you. You weren't in, so I left my name and number. You didn't call me back."

"I didn't know."

"I couldn't wait. All the flights were already booked, so I rented a car. I made it to the church one hour before the ceremony. But with the time change between New York and Chicago, I wasn't on time. I walked in just as the minister pronounced you man and wife. I was too late. I had lost you." His voice broke.

"That's so surreal. I watched for you. Hoping. Remember? I told you that."This is what she waited for; Simon to rescue her from another grand life mistake. He was too late, and she never saw him.

"That's why I'm telling you this now."

"Simon, we lost so much time. Years. Decades. And now we are left here, with just a pile of stupid dating stories."

"Only a pile of dating stories? Stupid stories?" He looked at his disappearing boner. "Maybe we weren't meant to be," he said, getting up to search for his pants.

"Where are you going?" Alice became deeply troubled.

"You married Thomas and had Zeba. Everything happens for the best." Finding his briefs, he stepped into them, catching the heel of his foot and nearly toppling over.

"For the best? Whoa. We just took a wrong turn there. Wait, don't go. Not yet."She yanked the sheet from her body and got up to challenge him to stay.

Alice's heart ached; her hands shook. She tried to smile but tasted only tears. Her heart stopped beating, it seemed. Her legs turned to jelly. No way would she allow Simon to get the better of her. She was getting out of this non-relationship at the right time—and just in time before she wasted the rest of her life on this guy."Our story is done, and so you have another story to tell. You just move along, don't you? It was never me." Alice rummaged through the desk drawer. She knew she wasn't coping well.

"What are you doing?"

"Ah, here it is, our contract. And here I am tearing

it up."

"Alice, stop. Just stop."

A crushing sorrow shook her—a sorrow she had never known. She threw the contract, now confetti, into his face. With that, she threw away her dreams. "I do not want your money."

"Look, I am exhausted." He rubbed his forehead. "There's another story I should be writing this moment instead of arguing with you. Where are my jeans?"

"Just like that, you're leaving me, again?"

"Alice, it's late and you drank too much. We've said too much."

"Always another story. You know what? I think you've just been stringing me along all these years just to make a buck." Why didn't she feel embarrassed standing naked in front of this man who was getting dressed because he no longer wanted to fuck her?

"You can't seriously believe that." Simon stuffed his socks in his jeans pockets and pulled on his shoes. Then he tried pulling his jeans on over his shoes. It didn't work.

"You need to—you need to remove your shoes first." She pointed.

"I know." He took off his shoes, put on his jeans, then slid back into his shoes. "So—what's next for us?"

Her heart beat wildly. Almost at the door now with Simon completely dressed, zipped, and buttoned, it felt like a train speeding over broken tracks. His feet were heavy on the steps down to the street where the door clicked closed.

Alice shivered uncontrollably as she reached the bathroom and turned on the shower spigot. Warm water and tears poured down her face, across her shoulders, over her collarbone, and down her body on its rush to the drain at her feet. Only an hour earlier, Simon had been standing in this very loft about to make love to her. Now she was alone, wallowing in grief, except for Jasper, who howled at her from the other side of the shower curtain.

She turned the spigot off and dried her skin slowly as though it would somehow heal her. Turning off the lights, she groped her way back into the couch sheets still wrapped in the towel. Jasper laid his head on her neck, perhaps sensing her deep sadness. "Are you used to cajoling sad women?"

"It wasn't supposed to turn out like this, Jasper. Not again. Simon was supposed to stay at least for the night, and then forever."The next wave of emotion hit her even harder and she burst into tears again until she could no longer breathe. Alice opened her heart and welcomed the hurt into her body. She wanted to experience each pang deeply no matter how many days or weeks or months or years it took to get over Simon. This time she would finally do it.

Chapter 34

Alice

In the coming days, she fielded calls from Simon. Thread by thread her life fell apart, one strand at a time. No one could really see that except her. Alice stared at herself in the mirror. She saw a woman who seemed self-confident, pulled together, intelligent. Good. That's how things were meant to look. She chose not to burden anyone with her heartbreak. Instead, she experienced the pain alone.

To top off her broken heart, there were months' worth of store receipts to pour over, an angry daughter, and a dear friend whose baby room she had to finish as soon as possible. Things were muddled—piled up to do. There was no more time for romantic thoughts of Simon. Every time she thought this might be their moment, the floor opened up.

This summer she found missing pieces and moments of herself in each person. It was like a puzzle finally coming together. And finally decided it didn't matter where the thread started, or how it began unraveling her. It only mattered where it ended. It ended with Simon. After him, there was no more. No one else. Not ever. She was enough—maybe not for him—but for her.

She looked out the window at the black sky each

night after work. She traveled thousands of miles and ended up coming home with one of the two people she had left with—Simon. Her love story began long ago on a March evening when the sky was filled with hues of color. The harbor had turned from blue to black. Lobster was consumed and too much wine was guzzled. She was young, about twenty-ish. A stranger to love. Seeing it then and remembering it now, it was as though seeing it through a veil rendering the memory imperfect with a not so happily ever after ending.

It made her wish that in her twenties and thirties, she had known to not rush her journey of life but to take her time. Get to know herself. Time changes who you are. Experiences come. You grow and learn. And then you find out the choices you made along the way weren't the ones the person you become in the end would have made.

And next came Charlie and then Thomas. The thought of being married to Thomas slipped into the present. The three of them, Thomas, Zeba, and she at the dining room table.

Little Zeba silently ate her spaghetti noodles.

Thomas silently stirred his decaf coffee with a silver spoon and then cut into his steak.

Alice silently wished she could scream with boredom.

I am thinking of ending things, she wanted to tell him. *I've been thinking about it for a long time now. Thoughts are true. Actions can be faked. Like the faux string of pearls, you gave to me on our wedding day.* Not that it mattered. But then she got a fake marriage, too. Pretense was everything.

"How was work today?" Alice asked as she did

each night at this time.

And just like each night at this time, he answered, "Fine. What did you do all day?" he asked in return.

"I made a grocery list. Carted Zeba to and from kindergarten. Oversaw the maid's cleaning."

"What did you learn in school today, Zeba?"

"I learned—I learned about the letter M and what starts with the letter M. Like moose and mommy and—"

"Money!" Thomas said.

"Money. Many money." Zeba giggled.

The silence returned except for the scraping of forks and knives against the China plates.

"I think I will go to my study. I have work to do that will take most of the evening." Thomas rose from his seat and disappeared down the hall.

Alice looked at the empty plates and used utensils stuck with food. Zeba got down from the table and ran to her room. Alice merely sat and watched the clock. She felt older with every sound of the tick-tock.

Chapter 35

Tea with Talia.
Christmas

She wore an oversized pink top that slumped down her shoulder. Talia's dark hair had been scooped up and plopped on the top of her head, held with two bobby pins. Small curls cascaded down the side of her head.

"I have something for you. Alice opened her purse and took out a handwritten check. Here. I'm refunding the money for the babies' room."

"Wha-at? Why?" Talia asked in surprise.

"The room wasn't finished in time, and certainly wasn't up to my standards. Zeba flaked out on you. I feel like I did too."

"Nonsense. And, it's done now. More beautifully than I imagined."

"For that I am thankful. Here. I insist. The next time you give me a room to do, I will see it from start to finish. Take the check so my conscious is satiated."

"What do you hear from Zeba, anything?" Talia asked, putting the check into her purse.

"Nothing. She asked me to give her time and space, and I am giving her that. At least I know where she is; at her dad's in Chicago. Where she always wanted to be." Alice lifted her shoulders. "Still blaming me for all her issues."

"Isn't that normal?"

"Perhaps for a teenager but a young woman?" Alice sighed.

"She has things to sort out. I'm sure she will be back. Eventually."

"Well, that's up to her. She's an adult and has her own path to choose. I hope she chooses wisely."

"Is she in therapy?"

"Yes—I believe she still is. That's one good thing. Plus, she gets to spend time with Thomas, which is very good for them both. I hope she doesn't make things difficult for his wife."

"But that's out of your hands."

"It is. And for once, I am allowing myself to be selfish. I'm tired of doing what others want, filling their expectations—doing what's best for them. It's time I get what I want."

"Tell me about Zeba's dad. You rarely mention him."

Alice sat still for a moment, reflectively. "I wanted to get away from him."

"Why?"

"I felt drained. He drained me. I no longer loved him on any level. Even the sound of him entering a room gave me the willies. I had to get away from his control, the misery that filled the large house, condescension—it was a trap of some kind. I yearned for my freedom to become myself again."

"Is that why you sidestep every man who has come into your life since then? You project those feelings."

"Maybe."

"You need to know your worth. You are a woman who has made life give you what you want. You knew your dreams were within reach, so you stepped out of bad relationships to become healthy. Putting your needs first isn't a bad thing, as long as you don't hurt someone along the way."

"There may have been casualties."

"You are hard on yourself. Do you know what I see when I look at you? A woman who raised a lovely, strong daughter basically on her own, who runs two businesses and who just bought her first home, without help from anyone. Someone who has oodles of friends. A gal who isn't afraid of putting her dating life out there so others might learn from her mistakes and faux pas. Most of all I see a woman who is terribly in love with Simon because he is the right choice."

"Simon, the right choice? For me? What did you just say?" Alice sat up straight.

"You raised a lovely—"

"No, your last sentence. The one about Simon."

"Simon is the right choice."

"Maybe once he was, but no more. By the way, I have news." She waved away the thought.

Talia looked excited to hear.

"I sold my shop." Alice beamed.

"To who, and why? I love your shop. What will I do now without you?"

"Hold on." Alice laughed. "Martin, Zeba's ex is back in town. I sold it to him because he wanted to start his own restaurant and it's in the perfect location. By helping him, I was able to help myself. Talia, I bought a warehouse for my finds. When I decorate homes, I now will have an array of selections to choose from no matter what the customer's style. It's my own business of design."

Talia fell back on the couch in laughter. "I am absolutely speechless! Good for you. And good for Martin, too."

"Yes, he's such a lovely man. I just hate that he and Zeba broke up. Well, it's none of my concern anymore. I'm just glad he got what he wants, and I do as well. My cottage now is going under renovations. Not an overhaul, but just a few things, like a big closet and a redo of the bathroom."

"I'm thrilled for you."

"I'm happy. Finally, I have real roots."

"By the way, have you heard from Simon?"

"Not for months. But I really didn't expect him to, not after our argument. I wonder when the book will be out."

"Now that you two are no longer together, how do you feel about Simon's book?" Talia reached for her iced tea.

"Conflicted." Alice picked up her glass along with a sugar cookie.

"How so?"

"Simon has been secretive about this. Always before, whenever he wrote about me on his blog, I had total approval of the piece first. Not so this time. The first time I'll see the book is when it hits store shelves. Makes me jittery."

"Why is he so cautious this time, do you suppose?"

"That's because we no longer speak. The trip. The book. It was the end of us. Finally. It had to happen sooner or later. There was no place for it to go." She bit into the cookie. "Hey, these are homemade. How do you find the time with the house and twin girls?"

"A nanny and a housekeeper. Luis picks up dinner

each night." She wiggled on the couch trying to find a comfortable position. "In a relationship, trust is a hard gift."

"Not for you."

"Oh yes, me too. There was a time when I wanted to run from my husband—before we were married that is."

"Run from Luis? But he is a gem."

"Yes, he remains a gem. Every doggone day. Do you know how aggravating it is to be married to the perfect man?"

Allice laughed at Talia, who batted a small pillow at her.

Talia continued. "It was me who had the doubts about lasting love. I was afraid that I would lose my artistic base for his overpowering nature."

"What changed?"

"I did. I relaxed. Allowed myself to fully and completely love and trust. I feel you have a distrust of men. Well, founded, I'm sure. But at some point, you must let that all go and start over, that is, if that's what you want. If you want Simon."

"Simon no longer wants me."

"I hear your strong words, but your voice sounds sad."

"It's been a long realization. I am not lucky at love. How do you manage?"

"Luis manages. And the days he doesn't manage so well, I do. We are close, but two separate people who share a home and babies and a life. We want this." She waved her arms about. "We want us. So we work at it. Sometimes the work is hard and other times it's positively delightful." She winked.

"I learned a lot about myself. I feel stronger as an individual, more centered. My perspective is clearer. And not just focused on Simon. I am focused on what makes me happy and fulfills me. And I suppose Simon is fulfilled and busy with Fiona now. We each got what we wanted."

"I've heard from Simon."

"Oh?" Alice sat forward eager to hear more. Realizing she looked too anxious she settled back into the couch trying to act nonchalant.

"Fiona is moving to Denton."

"They are marrying?"

"Oh no, definitely not. Simon is renting his condo to her."

"Where will he live?" Alice took a sip of green tea and tried not to gag.

"Simon is looking to buy a house. He hopes to get one on Oak Street."

"One of the historic districts. Interesting." Trying to lighten the negativity she suddenly felt, she jokingly added, "Well, if you hear he needs an interior designer, give him my card."

Talia looked a bit uneasy as she shifted in her wicker chair. "Simon came to dinner last night. Alone. No, 'plus one'. Luis forbids me to question him about you. Now don't take it personally. He just didn't want to make him feel uncomfortable."

"I don't trust Simon."

"And that is because you thought he was with Fiona?"

"It's way more complicated than that. I've known him for over half my life, and it seems just as we get close, he dances away from me. I'm tired of it. What else did Simon have to say?"

"He's excited about the book, but said it took an unexpected turn."

"Did he mention what that was?"

"Didn't say anything more, although I tried to pry it from him."

"I worry about how it's framed."

"Not to change the subject, but I have someone I want you to meet."

"Oh no. I am done with all of that. No more fix-ups, meet-ups, or faux dates." Alice waved her off. "Blanche has officially gone into retirement."

"Just hear me out, okay?"

"Why?"

"Because I am your friend and you have to trust me. Do you?"

"Yes, I do trust you."

"Then do it for me? Just this once. Please."

"I don't know." Alice's forehead wrinkled as she shook her head.

"Just so you know, I will pester you until you give in."

"Oh, all right. But only for the sake of my sanity."

"Good. You will meet him at Barley and Board tonight at seven." Talia walked Alice to the door.

"Thank you for always being there for me. As you say, Simon has a surprise about his book that I have yet to see, but I have an even bigger surprise for him that he'll never see coming."

Chapter 36

Simon
The date

"You stood me up," were the first words Simon said when she opened the door.

"Yes, I did." Alice grabbed the edge of the door as Jasper stuck his nose out between her legs to see who was at the door. "I walked into the restaurant and saw my 'fix-up' was you. Don't look so infuriated. I've done this before. Walked out on men I didn't care to meet. Surely you remember that from the dating blog."

"Yeah, but this time it was me." His voice cracked and seemed to crumble into pieces.

"Bravo. It's good to empathize with your book's characters." Alice opened the door wider. "You may come in."

"Do you know how long it took me to find you here?" he asked, crossing the threshold.

"Don't be so dramatic. I'm sure Talia gave you my address." She rolled her eyes.

"Have a seat?" She pointed toward the couch and took a nearby armchair.

Simon looked around at the small room flanked in shiplap and painted white. Large framed vintage pictures of cranes and botanicals warmed the space.

"Hey, Jasper, how are you, boy?" He rubbed his

ears.

"I can tell he remembers you by all his wiggling and crying."

"That's cos I'm unforgettable." Simon then held out a wrapped gift which Alice eagerly accepted.

"If this is what I think it is, I can't wait to see it." Alice removed the paper from around the book while he did his best to pretend he wasn't anxious about her reaction.

The wrapping paper bow lay at her feet and she held the book. Simon remained silent while Alice studied the dust cover.

Had she forgiven him? Was she upset over the new title? Annoyance was his knee-jerk reaction.

"Oh my, it's the book. It's so large, like a coffee table book. I never expected that." She fanned the pages and seemed to marvel at large black and white, some in color, pictures of the summer trip.

Finally, he assumed Alice was pleased by her smile and her eyes that lit up.

Simon watched as she turned it over and over in her hands rubbing her fingers on it and feeling its weight. "The book itself is such a shiny off cover while the dust cover is sure to stop the customer in their tracks. Amazing. All of this. I had no idea. The three of us, Megan, Fiona, and myself building that snowman."

"Phew. I am so relieved you like it. I chose that particular photograph because it was the start to building a friendship. You three had a lot of shit to figure out but you all did just that. Alice, I know I said it was your story but it ended up so much more. I think it's a story of three strong women who chose different paths but became friends during a hard journey."

"That's the title. *A Hard Journey into the Past to Save the Future*."

"There's something I want you to see first, look at the front of the book. Just inside the cover. I wrote something to you." He stood and turned the page so she wouldn't miss it.

"I ask you to breathe in, and keep these words close, like a wish, or press your ear against a seashell hearing the ocean as I speak to you. Put me in a maze and watch me find my way out to you. Or stroll into my being and find the latch. I want to dance through life with you into the deep ocean as you call my name."

Alice held back tears. "Who is that for?"

"I already said. Look at the dedication." Her eyes fluttered in tears and read: "To my Alice."

"How beautiful. It's touching." She held her hand against her chest. Her voice was hardly a whisper. "Thank you. And I love the first page of the old church where you first met Fiona. It seems showcased, but rightly so. There's no way you can tell it's a church from the angle. Just looks like a neat old building. And you superimposed me onto it with Fiona and Megan too. I am speechless. I will spend many hours reading the stories of the three of us and admiring your photographs."

"I am so relieved you aren't pissed off at me."

"Fiona? How is she these days?"Alice said her name without a tone of malice.

"Good. Starting over is never easy." Now he began to feel jittery again as silence dropped between them. "Hey, about this place. Tell me."

"It's mine. All mine." She beamed, setting the book on the old English teacart next to where she sat.

The warm afternoon sun streamed into the room setting her face aglow with sprinkles of what seemed like fairy dust. Her eyes were warm reflecting peace.

Dare he take her into his arms and tell her how happy he was for her? And wow, look at this place. She did it, all by herself. How? The fireplace made of stucco and shaped as an oval was painted white. The original floors were worm wood and the barnwood arched beamed ceiling was really nice. Large Navajo rugs in various hues of browns, reds, and pinks as well as sizes stretched across the old floors. Certain she had hand-picked each piece of furniture, he had to know. "Did a rich uncle die?"

"One didn't have to. Two things made it possible. The first is, I sold my shop. To Martin. Never knew the building was worth so much money."

"I for one certainly never would have guessed. What's number two?"

She gave a look of contentment and Simon knew she wasn't ready to disclose that secret.

"Okay. What's next for you?" he asked.

"I'm starting my own design business. So much to do and to learn." Alice sprang to her feet. "There's a studio out back where I keep my art books and samples stored. There is even a little room above for me to refurnish furniture. But not antiques. Never touch old original wood with paint. I only clean those up."

"No doubt you will be totally successful." This was the former Alice he remembered from college days. That Alice was back. Plus ten times more interesting than ever.

"What a nice thing to say. Come on, let me show you around this place."

In her bedroom, he stood at the foot of her bed and imagined her resting there. A large shag rug was centered in the room over the old wood boards. The bed looked plenty comfortable, with layered covers starting in white, then added more texture with gray woolen blankets and red patterned throws. A few large pillows were well placed. A side table flanked each side and had mismatched but charming old large lamps to read by no matter which side she decided to sleep. Her desk was placed by the window and her laptop was open as though she had been busy working when the doorbell rang.

"Look at this, will you?" She opened an oak sliding door.

"Wow, it's rare to see a walk-in closet in a vintage home." Simon stepped into the space.

"I knocked out a wall. Rather, I had a wall knocked out. I indulged." Alice leaned against the doorjamb.

"I see that." Simon counted his steps. "Ten by fifteen?"

She nodded.

"I've seen bigger, but this is great for you. Nice built-in drawers too." He walked from one side to the other in less than ten steps. The hangers hung with equal distance from one to the other. He laughed. She had arranged the clothes by blouses, pants, and dresses; then by color.

"Eventually I'll buy more clothes, but for now, just spreading them out. Go ahead, look in my drawers."

"You want me to." He stated with a laugh, tugging at her jeans.

"I know *you* want to." She ignored his obvious attempt and then pulled out the top drawer.

Underwear was carefully folded and placed one on top of the other in neat rows. Stockings rolled into a ball and tucked into a corner. Socks of all colors were doubled over in pairs. Next drawer, bras folded and arranged. The third drawer contained jewelry packed with Native American turquoise pieces and Mexican sterling, many with Hubble beads. There seemed to be no space to add more.

Alice's gaze remained on him. It made him uncomfortable because he had come to say so much. He was ready to empty his heart to her. Now his words melted away. Would he be able to remember them? The worry made him tense. He was talking a lot, but not about the important stuff. Feelings were hard for him to say. In the past, he always ran when it was time to express them. Alice found it easy to talk about feelings as though it was a recipe she was reciting. Not Simon. He ran.

"My bathroom is nice too." She pointed across the room in the opposite direction.

"And the bathroom is out this way?" He hated it sounded lame and empty.

She pointed again. "It's a small house, Simon. You are bound to locate it sooner or later."

He crossed her bedroom and peeked into the bathroom. "Nice shower and tub. Marble."

"Thanks."

Back in the bedroom, he walked in a circle around the bedroom.

"Nice chair." He touched the cushioning on the tufted armchair and then looked out the window musing to himself that it was a really great neighborhood. The peace and quiet alone was priceless. "Your yard is big enough for a dog."

"My bed is really comfortable. No more fold-out couch for me—not ever." She laughed and swept her hair back behind her ears as she sat at the edge, signaling with a wave of the hand to join her.

At the edge of the bed was a crocheted quilt. The bedside table held a picture of Zeba as a little girl. "How are things going with her?"

"She's very mad at me again. Most likely for helping Martin. Won't answer my calls."

Simon sat next to Alice and put his hand on her shoulders. "She'll come home again. You'll see."

"I suppose you're right."

"Of course, I am. Sometimes you don't hear from certain people because they are on their journey figuring out things. Give it time." He bounced on the mattress a little. "Meanwhile, I'm happy for you. Your dream of house ownership has come true. But I still don't understand how that shop could pay for all of this and plus a new business. Don't you need money for inventory?"

"Thank you, Simon. You made all this possible."

"I didn't do anything. You never cashed my check." He felt his mood slowly change.

She looked at him. Simon nodded as though there was an unspoken sentence that crossed between them right before she crumbled into his arms. Alice cried and Simon held her closer. He felt her breasts press into his chest. When she tried to wiggle away, he didn't allow it. Alice looked at him and he saw her eyes were glossy and her cheeks flushed.

Simon wanted to say more but was concerned he would say the wrong thing. "Talk to me."

"Oh, my goodness," Alice half laughed. "What's wrong with me? I feel so emotional."

Holding her, he suddenly understood her passion for being in her own space, for needing to love and to be loved. To feel safe and sheltered. Why hadn't he ever seen it? Over the years, all she talked about was the dream of her own home, to grow roots and a garden, paint her own walls, and not the crowded walls of a small loft.

"Would you like for me to show you my garden?" She pulled back and looked at him.

"No, not right now, anyway." Simon's voice was soft, and he kissed her neck. Her cheek. Her chin. She trembled. He stopped and looked again into her eyes. He kissed her eyelids closed. Alice became quiet. Unmoving. Still. He only detected the rise and fall of her chest.

Then his lips pressed against hers. Tender nibbles and Alice gasped, then sighed as he squeezed her knee.

"Simon." She locked her gaze on him.

"Sssh. It's okay. Everything is fine."

He laid back on the bed and pulled her to him. She got on top of him and pressed her groin into him. Relief washed; glad she wanted him too. It suddenly seemed good and right. They were here alone in her little home, the home she always wanted. Perhaps now she would feel she belonged and didn't need her past so much. Maybe here they could reconcile their past, in order to have a present and future.

His entire being filled with lust, not remembering when he wanted anyone as much as he wanted Alice. He loved how she worked her lower body against him, making him harder and harder. "Hey, baby." He pulled off her top and unsnapped her bra. It fell between them.

Alice grabbed for it. "Simon, it's been so long. I don't look the same."

"I don't either. Look." He opened his pants to show her.

They laughed.

She slid off to the side to unbutton his shirt, kissing his skin as she traveled south, mapping every scar and freckle. When she reached the snaps on his jeans, Simon flipped Alice onto her back and ran his fingers over her freckles and around her nipples. After burying his face in her breasts, he opened his mouth to suck her right nipple but couldn't find it. He opened his eyes and searched. It was there a moment ago.

Alice tapped him on the shoulder. "You can find them here on the side under my armpit when I lay on my back." She pressed the outer edge of her breasts together forming a volcano-type rise. "See? Back in place."

They laughed hysterically as Simon wrapped her up in his arms and held her skin against his bare chest. Alice pressed her head into the nook of his shoulder. It felt so good and right being here with her, the woman who was always the focus of his life. It had to take a trip into her past to find her. "You are so beautiful, Alice."

Alice reached between them and slowly unzipped his pants. She pressed her hand between his skivvies and his skin, grabbing hold of his cock which made him groan loudly. She wrapped her hand around him and slowly pumped. Feeling his nuts contract and get rock hard, all he could think about was how good it was going to feel once he got inside of her. Simon leaped from the bed and kicked off his pants. Leaning over Alice, he jerked off her pants, flinging them behind him. Just as quickly, he got on top of her and as Alice parted her legs she yelled in pain.

"What's wrong? What did I do?"

"You did nothing. It's my damn hip again. Let me readjust myself." After a few shifts of her body on the mattress and a pillow, she said, "Ready."

Going slowly was important to him, but his overwhelming desire to be inside her made it impossible to resist. He entered her with a forceful push. She gasped and jumped a little.

"Did that hurt?" he asked softly.

She shook her head.

He thrust, riding her back and forth. She quivered and moaned. The intensity grew until she was holding him against her tightly and raising her hips as she swayed from side to side. As a loud moan escaped her, he heard himself cry out with pleasure.

Chapter 37

Alice

Why had she fallen asleep? In the meantime, had Simon made another escape? There was an empty space where he left his imprint on the bedsheets. The cottage was eerily still. She sat up but didn't see his cast-off clothes. Quickly she pulled on a light robe just as the doorbell rang. There were footsteps, the sound of a door opening followed by Simon's voice.

"Food," he called out. "Are you still asleep?"

There was his face in the door frame. She brightened. "What did you have delivered?"

"Pizza, of course."

"No hot wings, too?"

They sat in the garden on iron chairs, eating pizza and drinking wine. Simon in his underpants and a sweatshirt, and Alice with a slip under an open kimono.

"What plans do you have for your loft?"

"Rent it out. If you hear of someone needing a small rental, send them my way."

"There is someone I have in mind."

"Surely not Fiona, she's renting your condo."

"So, you've been brought up to snuff by talking to Talia. Yes, Fiona is renting to buy. And it just so happens, I do know someone who wants it if the rent is reasonable."

"In this market, I can name my price even with the one bedroom. You know someone?"

He nodded.

"Is it Zeba? Is she coming home? Surely, she would never want to live there again, but if so, I can have it completely renovated."

Simon took her hand and held it. "Calm down. Not Zeba. It's—Megan."

Alice's hand flew up to her mouth. "You've heard from her? Oh my gosh, how is she?"

"Seems like both your new best friends are coming to town to live." Simon laughed. "Fiona in the condo, and Megan needs a place to live with her baby."

"Boy or girl?"

"Boy."

"I will renovate the place for Megan and her child. When? When do they arrive? And what about Charlie?"

"Seems like Charlie isn't ready for fatherhood and took off."

"How awful. She is going to need lots of support. Oh dear, I wonder if she will want Jasper back." Hearing his name, he stood and walked to Alice looking for a handout.

"Not if the landlord doesn't permit pets in the loft, then you have nothing to worry about."

Alice laughed. Since being with Simon seemed so easy at the moment, she gathered her threadbare nerves to open up to Simon. "There are some things that need saying."

"Oh boy. Am I in trouble?" Eyebrows raised.

She touched his hand and circled a spot with her fingers. "You shouldn't have taken me to Corpus, Simon. Our time there made me fall in love with you."

"Whaaaat? Why are you bringing this up now? Wasn't this a conversation meant for about thirty or more years ago?"

"You had no intention of loving me back." Alice dove in. "You played me. Do you know how unfair that was especially to a young girl?"

"You've been carrying this around all this time? Without saying a word?" Simon asked.

"My timing sucks but I need to have this conversation with you."

"All right then. Let's have it. You've got it all wrong, Alice. I did love you. I was too young and didn't know how to handle my feelings, so I ran."

"You loved me?" The thought never occurred to her.

"Of course, I loved you. I've never stopped. It was impossible to get over you so that's why I started calling after I left. Why do you think I moved from New York City to live in Denton, Texas?"

"Tell me. I need to hear you say it."

"I wanted to be close to you and Zeba."

"You sure are good at holding back feelings. I thought we were only friends all this time."

"We've been lovers. And we've been friends."

"What are we now?"

"We are friends. Best friends. Partners. And I would like more of this." He nodded toward the bedroom.

"Here we sit over pizza and wine, a lifetime later. Your imprint is on my life. I've carried such passion for you all these years that it now stains who I am."

"Alice, you're like one of those romance novels, aren't you? You need to write one. I think you'd be good at it."

Forty-seven separate thoughts spun. Alice scrunched her eyes closed thinking of the possibility of love after all with this man. Memory cells came alive and tingled through her being. Hopeful thoughts flooded. She didn't try to make sense of any of it—just wanted to feel it unfold. Her life had been a fabric with various colors and patterns. He was saying he loved her. Simon was hers for the taking. She was taken at this moment by how bold and self-assured he was about them. He had never been quite like this before. The men who trampled through her life before Simon and post-Simon had been all flash, no substance. A light feeling came over her. The evening porch light above them flickered on.

"Are you all right? Alice? Alice."

The sound of his voice saying her name, in that familiar timbre, swept through her like a spring breeze. It made her lungs pull a sharp breath as her forearm hair prickled. For a timeless moment, she remained frozen, locked into temporary silence. With her heart so full, she didn't want to come to her senses. To think of all the reasons why she should turn and run into the house for refuge, forgetting Simon once and for all.

But her senses reeled. Her heart opened. The truth was, she wanted him. Wanted to cook him dinner, wanted to wash his back in the shower, wanted his shoulder to cry on, his ear to listen to her fears, his arms that would hold her. Most of all she wanted to lie down with him at night and wake up with him each morning. Should she risk it, just one more time? But there was one thing she would not do.

Alice eased closer to Simon, wondering what to

say next. She needed words that would unite them. Nervousness bubbled, resulting in shaking hands. Perhaps this was her last moment. Her last chance to set things right. If she didn't do it now, she might live the rest of her life with deep regret.

Alice made a fist, wanting to smack back the fear—not wanting to be rejected. But the great love that rushed ashore many years ago in Corpus and the growing love that deepened over the years settled back into the folds of her heart. It was a part of her and would be forever.

"Tell me what you need to say to me and what you need from me," he said, stroking Alice's fist, forcing her to relax her fingers—threading his through hers.

"Simon." She expected her dazed confusion to fill his eyes with tenderness, but what she saw was a flash of dread. Not the kind of dread when the restaurant bill was too high, or when he found the scratch on the driver's side of his car, but dread of being turned away. She figured he was misunderstanding her hesitancy.

She'd never been one to trust easily when it came to men, but there was a new sincerity in Simon's eyes, one she had never seen before. Suddenly everything about him seemed safe. Now it was her turn to make him feel safe. Alice called love from the foggy place that she had sent away time and again.

His hand felt strong and protective over hers, and she saw in his eyes a longing to be close to her again. She wanted him too. Wanted him forever. A tiny exhale escaped her as she expelled the tremendous pull of desire to be held and loved by Simon.

Alice looked him in the eyes. "If what you say is true, then I need for you to stay. Forsaking all others."

"Forsaking all others," he repeated. "I want to stay with you for always."

"For always you may stay."

"I will stay but I need to ask you something."

"I'm listening."

"Let's get married.'"

"Whoa, That was totally unexpected." Alice fidgeted with the edge of her napkin.

He said it so fast that Alice expected him to laugh and admit he was joking. But seconds ticked past, and he didn't laugh. Alice only coughed to hide the breath he had stolen from her.

"Marry me, Alice," he repeated.

Alice stared at him open-mouthed, not daring to picture herself as the blissful wife of this wonderful man. Salty tears gathered in the corners of her eyes. He kissed them away. "I love you. I know you love me, but it would sure be nice to hear it."

Just because she loved him didn't mean she was entitled to happiness with him. The unanswered proposal dangled between them like a gift she was too afraid to reach out and take. And then she knew what she would say.

"Yes—of course, I love you. But I can't say yes to marrying you."

"This is a joke, right?"

"Until this moment I never thought it possible you loved me too. I only hoped one day you would."

"Then I don't understand why you won't marry me."

"It's not that I don't want to marry you. I do want to be with you. And see you every day. And text and call. Date. Have wonderful sex with you as much and as long as we are able—especially with this bad hip of mine. But we've both been single for a very long time: me for over twenty years and you've never married. We are older now. No need to marry. We can be us, right here and now, and forever."

"This is hard to hear, but rather intriguing at the same time. I fell in love with you the first time I heard you with all that decorating talk." He laughed.

"You are such a liar. I know you pretend to be interested but you'd rather be anywhere else." She playfully nudged him.

"Seriously, you carry guilt of the past. Let me ask you a question that I asked someone else over a year ago. Tell me about your oldest friend and how you met."

"I met my oldest friend when he sat naked in my art class."

"If you got to relive that day, would you leave it as is or change it?" Simon thought about the people he asked this to. Now it was Alice's turn.

"I still wouldn't go for coffee with you."

"Why not?"

"Bad pickup line. I preferred our conversations in the donut shop."

"You say you carry guilt from the past. I carry guilt too, Alice."

"Guilt? What do you feel guilty about?" A niggling nervousness settled in her chest as tears crept over her bottom lids and spilled down her cheeks.

"For leaving you." He threaded his fingers through hers.

"Your job requires you to travel."

Now he chuckled, but just a bit. "That's not what I

mean, honey."

She squeezed his fingers. "Then tell me."

"Years ago, when I left for New York, I knew I was making a big mistake leaving you behind. But I wasn't brave enough to do anything about it. I had a broken-down car and a twenty-dollar bill in my pocket. My credit card had a three-hundred-dollar credit limit, and I had used two hundred and fifty of it."

She laughed a bit and tapped away the wetness on her face. Then her hip reminded her of the romp they just enjoyed. It wasn't pleased, although another body part had been pleased quite nicely. This moment was the most important of her life and she needed to hear each word clearly, and to understand what he meant.

Simon's lips flattened to a straight thin line and his words became soft and weightless. "I've been a coward when it came to you. I hurt you and was damn afraid I'd hurt you again."

"What's so different now?"

"I'm no longer a coward. I'll never leave you. Married or unmarried, I promise I won't leave."

He smoothed a curl that fell across her forehead. "You were my first and last love. My only love. So, are you sure you won't marry me?"

"I need time to get used to us." She leaned back in her chair and shivered. The evening air had a light chill. "We've always been together on some level but not the way we are now. Our relationship has been a roller coaster ride. I just want to be us without any label without any goal in mind. I've been in a hurry all my life. Hurried to forget you. Hurried to get married to my first husband. Hurried to be married the second time. Hurried to be a mom. Hurried to go to college. I need to slow down and enjoy the now."

"The first marriage was probably a rebound from thinking you lost me." Simon kissed the back of her hand.

"If that was a rebound marriage then what was the second?"

"Your practice marriage. Ours will be a real marriage."

"Your words are just air to me right now. Let it breathe. Let it grow."

"Where will we live?" He looked around at the small bungalow.

"You will live at your place." She shrugged.

"Ah, I don't have a place, remember? Fiona is in my condo, and Megan has dibs on the loft."

"You can stay here until you find the right fit. But this is my place. My space to do with as I will. I can paint any wall I want, in any color I want, at any time of the day or night that I want. You owe yourself that freedom too. Believe me, marriage isn't all that great, at least not for me."

"I just need a day or two to adjust to this new idea. I thought when you fall in love then marriage is the next step."

"It can be. What we have between us right now in this moment is so good. Simon, I do love you. I have loved you since the beginning and have yearned for you all these years. I love you. That will never end. Only lately, I found I also love my independence. I am not discounting marriage, but I want to get used to this situation."

"Are these just excuses or does it have something to do with Jack and—"

Alice covered his mouth. "We shall never speak of any of them again. You also are not allowed to blog about them again either. We need a new blog, new stories."

"Yeah, my book kind of killed that storyline."

"Just a little while ago you asked about the second thing that helped me buy both my new business and my home."

"You won the lottery." He joked with a wink.

"Nope. I sold a book." Alice stood and walked into the house and returned with an envelope. "I was paid a lot for it."

"I knew there was something you were keeping from me. Don't tell me you found a rare first edition. Who's the author?" He reached for the envelope.

"Me. I am the author of my own book."

"You? You wrote a book?"

"Indeed. I wrote a book." Alice poured herself another glass of wine and drank it down.

"Lots of people write books. But most of them are tossed in the slush pile. Only lucky people are offered a contract. However, you said your book made you money? Or are you hoping it will make you money once you find an agent?" Simon slowly measured his words as he opened the envelope and unfolded the paper.

"I found an agent."

"Who?"

"Yours."

"You contracted my agent?" Simon's jaw dropped as he read.

"And my publisher too?"

"Lucky me."

Simon ran his hand over the top of his head as he read the contract.

"I am waiting for the first edits. I am really excited to see them. Maybe you can give me some pointers."

"You never mentioned a book. When did you write this book?"

"I started writing on our road trip last summer, at the same time when you were snapping all those photographs and telling Megan, Fiona, and I to be nice to one another. I thought, if you can write a book, so can I. And I did, which included a tidy advance."

Simon continued to read.

Dinner for Two

A Guide to Faux Online Dating.

Tagline: An online tale of deception, lust, and confusion, while ferreting out the perfect guy.

Chapter 38

Simon's Last Dating Blog
The End of Blanche
Denton, Texas

For over half my life, I have written about Alice Rigby—disguised cleverly as someone by the name of Blanche. I've taken you on a journey of her dating life; good and bad, but always entertaining. In turn, I have been a silent bystander watching and writing from afar, trying to be objective in what she tells me, so I can weave her story in the town where she lives.

I am grateful for this moment. The tick of a clock—soaking in this moment. Thankful to at last have my eyes and heart open, to be wide awake, flourishing and fully alive. My life. So big. So small. So amazing—fragile and full. I am madly in love with Alice Rigby. And you will be hearing more from us in the not-so-far future. I popped the marriage question, and she finally said yes. Stay tuned. We have just started this new chapter. And more to add to our happily-ever-ending life together.

A word about the author...

Fascinated with stories, I began my writing career at the age of ten in the fifth grade. My first publication was during college. I received two dollars for my poem about a dog I rescued. Now as a retired teacher, I can't stop writing. Teaching, writing, gardening, and exploring are my passions. I live in Dallas with my two rescue dogs.

My books can be found under two names: Robin Shope and Robin Jansen

Friend me on Facebook.